RITES OF COMPASSION

Other books in the 2X2 series:

RITES OF COMPASSION

—

WILLA CATHER AND
GUSTAVE FLAUBERT

WITH AN INTRODUCTION BY
MARY GORDON

The Feminist Press
at the City University of New York
New York

Published in 2007 by The Feminist Press at the City University of New York,
The Graduate Center, 365 Fifth Avenue, Suite 5406, New York, NY 10016

Library of Congress Cataloging-in-Publication Data

Rites of compassion / Willa Cather and Gustave Flaubert ; with an introduction by
Mary Gordon.
     p. cm. — (2x2 series)
  ISBN-13: 978-1-55861-562-5 (pbk.)
  ISBN-10: 1-55861-562-8 (pbk.)
  I. Cather, Willa, 1873-1947. Old Mrs. Harris. II. Flaubert, Gustave, 1821-1880.
Cœur simple. English.
  PS643.R58 2007
  813'.52—dc22

                                    2007021438

Text and cover design by Lisa Force
Printed in Canada

13 12 11 10 09 08 07   5 4 3 2 1

CONTENTS

—

INTRODUCTION

—

Like all great works of fiction, "Old Mrs. Harris" and "A Simple Heart" make, on their readers, radical demands. They apply a pressure that creates a crack in the smooth surface of our understanding, a crack through which the light of new understanding enters and pervades. The subject matter of these two fictions, and the implications of the authors' treatment of their subjects, insist that we as readers rethink what Flaubert would call our "received ideas." Each generation has its own set of these, and our set, we readers of the first decade of the twenty-first century, is particularly challenged by these two works. For what ideas are more dearly held by us now than the importance of youth, sexual fulfillment, financial prosperity, personal agency? If these are our cardinal virtues, among the greatest of our capital sins is being taking advantage of. Not looking out for number one is a capital sin because we are all capitalists of personal happiness. We watch our hearts' investments like broody hens, determined that we not spend more than we earn, that we not squander what could, with careful husbandry, be making interest. The notion of sheer gift, given for its own sake and without thought of return, seems in our psychological landscape, the sheerest folly. Against this system of comprehension, Cather and Flaubert present us with two old women whose fulfillment is almost mystical in the completeness of its lineaments—despite the fact that it could very properly be said of them that they are used, even ill used, by the people they serve and live among.

Both Flaubert and Cather are masters of the tradition of realistic fiction, and their methods and preoccupations root themselves there. The stories are separated by over fifty years: "Un Coeur Simple" was written in 1876 and "Old Mrs. Harris" in 1930, but their formal and strategic similarities belie their temporal distance. We gather important information about the inner lives of characters through the details of the physical worlds that surround them; Flaubert considered this task of observation and notation a writer's most sacred obligation. The son of a doctor, Flaubert was devoted to an almost scientific precision of observation, observation from a distant, un-involved vantage point.

For Cather, this devotion to precision was essential. In *The Novel Démeublé*, Cather notes the importance of the novel's powers of observation, but also—perhaps more important, her own power of selection: "Is not realism, more than it is anything else, an attitude of mind on the part of the writer toward his material, a vague indication of the sympathy and candor with which he accepts, rather than chooses his theme" (1922). This integration of detail into the larger purposes of making the character known to us in all her fullness, is remarkably accomplished by both Flaubert and Cather in their descriptions of Félicité's and Mrs. Harris's physical surroundings.

Ford Madox Ford, one of Flaubert's most devoted disciples, said of this description that begins Flaubert's novella: "If you read these sentences with humility and attention . . . you will know more of France than if you spend months and months and months in one of the large hotels near the Tuileries gardens" (Stang 1986, 180):

> This house had a slate roof and stood between an alley and a lane that went down to the river. There was an unevenness in the levels of the rooms which made you stumble. A narrow hall divided the kitchen from the "parlor" where Mme. Aubain spent her day, sitting in a wicker easy chair by the window. Against the panels, which were painted white, was a row of eight mahogany chairs. On an old piano under the barometer a heap of wooden and cardboard boxes rose like a pyramid. A stuffed armchair stood on either side of the Louis-Quinze chimneypiece, which was in yellow marble with a clock in the middle of it modeled like a temple of Vesta. The whole room was a little musty, as the floor was lower than the garden.

The first floor began with "Madame's" room: very large, with a pale-flower wallpaper and a portrait of "Monsieur" as a dandy of the period. It led to a smaller room, where there were two children's cots without mattresses. Next came the drawing room, which was always shut up and full of furniture covered with sheets. Then there was a corridor leading to a study. The shelves of a large bookcase were respectably lined with books and papers, and its three wings surrounded a broad writing table in darkwood. The two panels at the end of the room were covered with pen-drawings, water-color landscapes, and engravings by Audran, all relics of better days and vanished splendor. Félicité's room on the top floor got its light from a dormer-window, which looked over the meadows. (106)

Near the beginning of *Old Mrs. Harris*, Cather describes Mrs. Harris's domain, her kitchen, from the point of view of Mrs. Rosen, the old woman's German Jewish neighbor:

It was a queer place to be having coffee, when Mrs. Rosen liked order and comeliness so much: a hideous, cluttered room, furnished with a rocking-horse, a sewing-machine, an empty baby-buggy. A walnut table stood against a blind window, piled high with old magazines and tattered books, and children's caps and coats. There was a wash-stand (two wash-stands, if you counted the oilcloth-covered box as one). A corner of the room was curtained off with some black-and-red-striped cotton goods, for a clothes closet. In another corner was the wooden lounge with a thin mattress and a red calico spread which was Grandma's bed. Beside it was her wooden rocking-chair, and the little splint-bottom chair with the legs sawed short on which her darning basket usually stood, but which Mrs. Rosen was now using for a tea-table. (29)

Later on in the story, Cather goes on to describe the following:

Her towel was hung on its special nail behind the curtain. Her soap she kept in a tin tobacco-box; the children's soap was in a crockery saucer. If her soap or towel got mixed up with the children's, Victoria was always sharp about it. The little rented house was much too small for the family, and Mrs. Harris and her "things" were almost required to be invisible. Two clean calico dresses hung in the curtained corner; another was on her back, and a fourth was in the wash. Behind the curtain there was always a good supply of aprons; Victoria bought them at church fairs, and it was a great satisfaction to Mrs. Harris to put on a clean one whenever she liked. (40–41)

How much is accomplished by these descriptions, and with what deftness Flaubert and Cather provide us with a wealth of information. From the description of chez Aubain, we understand the pretensions of the nineteenth-century French provincial bourgeois: the Louis Quinze style mantelpiece, the temple of Vesta, the picture of Monsieur in fanciful attire, the etchings meant to suggest more prosperous days. It is suggested, however, that the financial outlay devoted to making a certain social point might have been better used in achieving domestic comfort: The room smells musty and the floors are constructed in a way that makes it easy to trip.

It is a very different room from Mrs. Harris's kitchen, where nothing is there merely for show. Ramshackle and unrefined, it is nevertheless a place where life happens naturally and easily: a life that includes children, animals—and the old.

So Flaubert and Cather expend their energies upon the descriptions of rooms, not for their own sake, but to create a social context. Both understand the importance of class and money in determining not only the shape of labor, but additionally the flavor of manners and the hierarchies of daily habit. Citizens of the nineteenth century, they have none of their younger descendents' scruples in mentioning exact cash amounts: In the first two paragraphs, we learn that Félicité's annual salary is one hundred francs, and that the income realized from the properties Mme. Aubain rents out is only five thousand francs a year. Cather informs us that the amount needed to send Mrs. Harris's granddaughter Vickie to college is the impossible sum of three hundred dollars.

Flaubert and Cather react differently to the rigidity of class structure in their rendering of Félicité's and old Mrs. Harris's situations. Not surprisingly, given his famously ferocious hostility to the structures of the French bourgeoisie, Flaubert ascribes no romance to Félicité's social situation. Her lack of power consistently allows those who have more power than she to treat her cruelly. That she accepts being treated as a cipher in no way obviates the brutality of the treatment. For the whole of her life, Félicité is understood to be a creature to be used: That she might have desires, or even preferences is never taken into account. When her father dies, her family leaves her to her fate: She is a luxury they can't afford, and she is turned out of her first employment after being falsely accused of having stolen thirty sous. Her suitor abandons her when a rich widow can be more useful to him: She can buy him out of military conscription.

Whereas Félicité does not articulate her social situation, Mrs. Harris has considered the topic, and has brooded upon the changing nature of her place in the social scheme:

> At home, back in Tennessee, her place in the family was not exceptional, but perfectly regular . . . in Tennessee there had been plenty of helpers. There was old Miss Sadie Crummer, who came to the house to spin and sew and mend; old Mrs. Smith, who always arrived to help at butchering- and

preserving-time; Lizzie, the colored girl, who did the washing and who ran in every day to help Mandy. There were plenty more, who came whenever one of Lizzie's bare-foot boys ran to fetch them. The hills were full of solitary old women, or women but slightly attached to some household, who were glad to come to Miz' Harris's for good food and a warm bed, and the little present that either Mrs. Harris or Victoria slipped into their carpet-sack when they went away.

To be sure, Mrs. Harris, and the other women of her age who managed their daughter's house, kept in the background; but it was their own background, and they ruled it jealously. They left the front porch and the parlor to the young married couple and their young friends; the old women spent most of their lives in the kitchen and pantries and back din-ing-room. But there they ordered life to their own taste, entertained their friends, dispensed charity, and heard the troubles of the poor. (61–62)

Mrs. Harris' understanding of the fixed nature of social hierarchy might be considered almost feudal; she doesn't for a moment consider the conditions of Mandy the "bound girl," or the "colored girl," who ranks even below Mandy. And Cather shares none of Flaubert's outrage at the cruelty of bourgeois employers; her outrage is saved for the West-ern democratic upstarts who don't understand the rules of the traditions of the Southern aristocratic way. But woven into the tapestry of tradition, like the deliberate error woven into Persian carpets to ward off the evil eye, is Mrs. Harris's deliberate upending of the ordinary sense of obligation the young owe the old. Her system seems to deliberately flout the fourth commandment: It is the young, particularly young women, who are to be honored by their elders. Honored for their very youth, and therefore served.

> "We are only young once, and trouble comes soon enough." Young girls, in the South, were supposed to be carefree and foolish; the fault Grandmother found in Vickie was that she wasn't foolish enough. When the foolish girl married and began to have children, everything else must give way to that. She must be humored and given the best of everything, because having children was hard on a woman, and it was the most important thing in the world. In Tennessee every young married woman in good circumstances had an older woman in the house, a mother or mother-in-law or an old aunt, who managed the household economies and directed the help. (61–62)

But considered in another light, Mrs. Harris's willingness to serve her young, beautiful daughter is an investment in the future; she understands the importance of an image of grace and ease to the possibilities of a rich life for her grandchildren—particularly her grandsons—whose simple affection is much less problematic than the tangled emotions of her daughter and granddaughter. Mrs. Harris's understanding of the importance of things that would be considered wasteful or useless differentiates her from her striving, middle-class neighbors, but binds her to the Rosens, the Jewish couple next door, where Mrs. Harris's bookish granddaughter, Vickie, goes to read and learn about the larger world.

In introducing Mrs. Rosen, Cather provides the perspective of the ultimate outsider. Not only is Mrs. Rosen not American; she is a Jew. Like Mrs. Harris, she seems to partake of a fineness that eludes the other characters in the story—particularly the townspeople they are forced to live among. Mrs. Harris's fineness is instinctual, inborn, whereas Mrs. Rosen's is the product of acquired civilization. Both women share a respect for formal standards, for rules kept whether or not anyone else is looking, whether or not anyone understands.

By including the complex character of Mrs. Rosen, Cather creates a masterful triangle which the three women precariously negotiate, a triangle of female understanding, jealousy, pride, and power. Mrs. Rosen envies Victoria's ease and grace; she admires her fecundity (she herself is infertile), maternal generosity, and imagination. But she harshly judges her carelessness and what she considers her abuse of her mother. Mrs. Harris values Mrs. Rosen's friendship, but understands that Victoria can't bear even a hint of criticism in her home, and resents any attentions paid to anyone except herself. And so, her friendship with Mrs. Rosen becomes a cause for anxiety. But she relies on Mrs. Rosen to provide access to the outer world for her granddaughter Vickie, an access that her daughter- and son-in-law, with all their Southern graces, cannot provide. All Mrs. Harris's connections render her a vessel for important female emotions, including some transgressive ones, such as ambition and shame.

It would be possible to assume that Mrs. Harris's life is more fortunate than Félicité's in that her situation seems her choice rather than an imposition. Rather than a servant at the mercy of her masters, her world is cushioned by the familial, particularly by the love of her young grandchildren. But Félicité is allowed a luxury that Mrs. Harris is denied: the luxury of tears. Twice, she collapses physically, overcome by weeping when the difficulty of her life is born upon her: once when her lover abandons her, and again when she is lashed by the whip of an impatient driver when she is on her way to get her beloved parrot stuffed.

Mrs. Harris does not permit herself to mourn over her losses even for a moment—as if it didn't occur to her that a more fortunate fate might have been hers. And the scene in which Cather describes Mrs. Harris's relationship to an old sweater indicates an impoverishment more extreme than any we observe in Félicité's experience:

> Although Mrs. Harris's lounge had no springs, only
> a thin cotton mattress between her and the wooden

slats, she usually went to sleep as soon as she was in bed. To be off her feet, to lie flat, to say over the psalm beginning: *"The Lord is my shepherd,"* was comfort enough. About four o'clock in the morning, however, she would begin to feel the hard slats under her, and the heaviness of the old home-made quilts, with weight but little warmth, on top of her. Then she would reach under her pillow for her little comforter (she called it that to herself) that Mrs. Rosen had given her. It was a tan sweater of very soft brushed wool, with one sleeve torn and ragged. . . .

She slipped it under her apron, carried it into the house with her, and concealed it under her mattress. There she had kept it ever since. She knew Mrs. Rosen understood how it was; that Victoria couldn't bear to have anything come into the house that was not for her to dispose of.

On winter nights, and even on summer nights after the cocks began to crow, Mrs. Harris often felt cold and lonely about the chest. Sometimes her cat, Blue Boy, would creep in beside her and warm that aching spot. But on spring and summer nights he was likely to be abroad skylarking, and this little sweater had become the dearest of Grandmother's few possessions. It was kinder to her, she used to think, as she wrapped it about her middle, than any of her own children had been. She had married at eighteen and had had eight children; but some died, and some were, as she said, scattered. (37–39)

But despite the hardships of their lives, neither Félicité nor Mrs. Harris possesses a shred of rebelliousness, and this shared characteristic erases the differences in their estates; that one is a servant and one a family member seems less important than their shared habits of stoic resignation. They are fatalistic, and both authors see their fatalism as a species of nobility—despite the fact that the tone of Flaubert's social criticism is much harsher than Cather's. The paradox of their fatalism is that while their Zen-like acceptance spares them the wasted energy of angry head-banging or breast-beating, it also frees them to turn their attention to the task at hand, and this attentiveness renders them masters of their métier of domestic life. Their mastery is noted by the larger community. *A Simple Heart*, for example, begins with a communal accolade; "Madame Aubain's servant Félicité was the envy of the ladies of Pont-l'Evêqe for half a century" (105).

Community appreciation of Mrs. Harris is more personalized. The town busybody uses her admiration for Mrs. Harris as a weapon to punish Victoria, whose youthful charm excites the jealousy of the local wives. Outside esteem for Mrs. Harris also takes a benign form in the admiration of Mrs. Rosen. But because the relationships are individual rather than simply typical, Mrs. Rosen's admiration for Mrs. Harris comes at a price.

Mrs. Harris had gathered from Mrs. Rosen's manner, and from comments she occasionally dropped, that the Jewish people had an altogether different attitude toward their old folks; therefore her friendship with this kind neighbor was almost disturbing as it was pleasant. She didn't want Mrs. Rosen to think she was "put upon," that there was anything unusual or pitiful in her lot. To be pitied was the deepest hurt anybody could know. And if Victoria once suspected Mrs. Rosen's indignation, it would be all over. She would freeze her neighbor out, and that friendly voice, that quick pleasant chatter with the little foreign twist, would thenceforth be heard only at a distance, in the alley-way or across the fence. Victoria had a good heart, but she was terribly proud and could not bear the least criticism. (39–40)

Paradoxically, perhaps, although Félicité is a domestic servant, the range of her admirable qualities extends farther to the outside world than Mrs. Harris's. She is able to control the drunken behavior of her employer's visitors, and she displays heroic physical courage and enormous intelligence in saving Mme. Aubain and her children from the onslaught of a raging bull. But Mrs. Harris, too, is not without courage. To ask a stranger for money—money which her son-in-law as head of the family ought to be able to provide, requires that Mrs. Harris set aside her treasured pride and break the circle of familial propriety. But she does this because it is the only way that her granddaughter Vickie can take advantage of the college scholarship that she has won. In understanding the importance of this, Mrs. Harris has to acknowledge the limitations of her way of life at a time when most people cling like death to the bark of their own assumptions.

An admiring tenderness—both Flaubert and Cather bestow this on their characters. Flaubert's tenderness is mixed with comedy; nevertheless his characteristic harshness is considerably softened in his portrait of Félicité. It was an impulse of tenderness that generated his writing of the story; he wrote it to please his beloved friend Georges Sand, who urged him to write something more sympathetic than his prior work. Those who are used to thinking of Flaubert as taking the author's position extolled by his disciple, James Joyce, who is known for having said, "The author should be like God, standing at the edge of the universe paring his nails," might be surprised by Flaubert's own evaluation of his relationship to Félicité:

> *A Simple Heart* is just the account of an obscure life, that of Félicité, a poor country girl, pious but mystical, quietly devoted, and as tender as fresh bread. She loves successively a man, her mistress, her mistress' children, a nephew, an old man she is taking care of, then her parrot. When the parrot dies she has him stuffed, and when she herself is dying, she confuses the parrot with the Holy Ghost. It's not at all ironic, as you suppose, but on the contrary, very serious and

very sad. I want to arouse people's pity, to make sen-
sitive souls weep, since I am one myself. (1975, 458)

Their impulses toward tenderness take different forms in
each of the fictions. To be sure, Flaubert mixes his tenderness with a nice pinch of Gallic salt; it is impossible not to be
amused at Félicité's miscomprehensions of the world. Unable
to abstract, she doesn't understand the concept of mapping:

Cigars—they made her imagine Havana as a place
where no one does anything but smoke, and there
was Victor moving among the Negroes in a cloud
of tobacco. Could you, she wondered, "in case you
needed," return by land? What was the distance
from Pont-l'Évêque? She questioned M. Bourais to
find out.

He reached for his atlas and began explaining the
longitudes; Félicité's consternation provoked a fine
pedantic smile. Finally he marked with his pencil a
black, imperceptible point in the indentations of an
oval spot, and said as he did so, "Here it is." She
bent over the map; the maze of colored lines wearied her eyes without conveying anything; and on
an invitation from Bourais to tell him her difficulty
she begged him to show her the house where Victor
was living. Bourais threw up his arms, sneezed, and
laughed immensely: a simplicity like hers was a positive joy. And Félicité did not understand the reason;

how could she when she expected, very likely, to see the actual image of her nephew—so stunted was her mind! (127)

But we are more on Félicité's side than Bourais's, and her mistake does nothing to reduce our admiration for her. Both Félicité and Mrs. Harris are linked by their authors to children and animals, and the effect is not to diminish them but to increase our appreciation for the fullness of their creaturely richness. Both of them read with and like children, and both have animals who serve as familiars: Mrs. Harris's cat and Félicité's parrot. The portrayal of the cat is, by comparison, straightforward; Blue is only a beloved pet; Loulou may or not be the Holy Ghost.

But perhaps the most striking differences in the portrayals is the difference in the presentation of the women's bodies. We barely know what Félicité looks like, and we are most close to Félicité's physicality when she is having what might be known as an "out of body experience" (perhaps an interesting moment of authorial identification on the part of the epileptic Flaubert), as in the moment of her confusion at the harbor when she has run ten miles to say goodbye to her nephew Victor:

When she arrived in front of the Calvary she took the turn to the right instead of the left, got lost in the timber-yards, and retraced her steps; some people to whom she spoke advised her to be quick. She went all round the harbor basin, full of ships, and knocked against hawsers; then the ground fell away, lights flashed across each other, and she thought her wits had left her, for she saw horses up in the sky. (124)

Similarly, we are close to Félicité's somatic perceptions as she approaches death and her sensual faculties desert her one by one.

But Mrs. Harris's closely observed bodily life is an essential element of her characterization. Most often in literature, the female body is described as a vessel of sexual desire: It is rendered in its youthful freshness, prized for its allure and suggestion of fecundity: The female in literature is most often the object of the libidinal male gaze. But the visual is not the most important way we apprehend Mrs. Harris's body; we know her body as it experiences heat and cold, fatigue and heaviness, physical aloneness:

The kitchen was hot and empty, full of the untempered afternoon sun. A door stood open into the next room; a cluttered, hideous room, yet somehow homely. There, beside a goods-box covered with figured oilcloth, stood an old woman in a brown calico dress, washing her hot face and neck at a tin basin. She stood with her feet wide apart, in an attitude of profound weariness. She started guiltily as the visitor entered. (26)

One of Mrs. Harris's truest moments of communication occurs when Mandy, the "bound girl" massages the dying old woman's legs:

"Pore soul!" murmured Mandy. She put Grandma's feet in the tub and, crouching beside it, slowly, slowly rubbed her swollen legs. Mandy was tired, too. Mrs. Harris sat in her nightcap and shawl, her hands crossed in her lap. She never asked for this greatest solace of the day; it was something that Mandy gave, who had nothing else to give. If there could be a comparison in absolutes, Mandy was the needier of the two,—but she was younger. The kitchen was quiet and full of shadow, with only the light from an old lantern. Neither spoke. Mrs. Harris dozed from comfort, and Mandy herself was half asleep as she performed one of the oldest rites of compassion. (37)

Both "A Simple Heart" and "Old Mrs. Harris" include the deaths of their characters as part of their life stories. But what follows these deaths, what follows from these deaths, and what retroactive meaning these deaths bestow on the lives that preceded them vary greatly with the two authors. The virulently atheistic anticlerical Flaubert gives more than a hint of transcendence—however ironic—at the moment of Félicité's death.

An azure vapor rose up into Félicité's room. Her nostrils met it; she inhaled it sensuously, mystically; and then closed her eyes. Her lips smiled. The beats of her heart lessened one by one, vaguer each time and softer, as a fountain sinks, an echo disappears; and when she sighed her last breath she thought she saw an opening in the heavens, and a gigantic parrot hovering above her head. (151)

This ending can be read two ways: either as a sign that a belief in the transcendent is as confused as mistaking the Holy Ghost for a worm-eaten parrot, or that we will be greeted after death by some version of whatever it was we most loved.

Like Flaubert, Cather moves back at the very end of her story to achieve a larger perspective. But whereas Flaubert, the atheist, suggests the transcendent, the church-going Cather implies that the meaning of a life is in its familial relationships: One transcends the limits of individual biography by the legacies of kinship:

Thus Mrs. Harris slipped out of the Templetons' story; but Victoria and Vickie still had to go on, to follow the long road that leads through things unguessed at and unforeseeable. When they are old, they will come closer and closer to Grandma Harris. They will think a great deal about her, and remember things they never noticed; and their lot will be more or less like hers. They will regret that they heeded her so little; but they, too, will look into the eager, unseeing eyes of young people and feel themselves alone. They will say to themselves: "I was heartless, because I was young and strong and wanted things so much. But now I know." (101)

But perhaps Cather's is the greater irony, for the female familial line that passes from Mrs. Harris to Vickie will end with her: Vickie, who is based on the young Willa Cather, will produce, like her creator, not babies, but books.

Mary Gordon
New York City
May 2007

WORKS CITED

Cather, Willa. 1922. *The Novel Démeublé*. New York: Republic Pub. Co.

Flaubert, Gustave. 1971–75. *Oevres complètes, vol. 15*. Paris: *Club de l'Honnête homme*.

Stang, Sondra J., ed. 1986. *The Ford Madox Ford Reader*. New York: Ecco Press.

WILLA CATHER

OLD MRS. HARRIS

—

I

Mrs. David Rosen, cross-stitch in hand, sat looking out of the window across her own green lawn to the ragged, sunburned back yard of her neighbors on the right. Occasionally she glanced anxiously over her shoulder toward her shining kitchen, with a black and white linoleum floor in big squares, like a marble pavement.

"Will dat woman never go?" she muttered impatiently, just under her breath. She spoke with a slight accent—it affected only her *th*'s, and, occasionally, the letter *v*. But people in Skyline thought this unfortunate, in a woman whose superiority they recognized.

Mrs. Rosen ran out to move the sprinkler to another spot on the lawn, and in doing so she saw what she had been waiting to see. From the house next door a tall, handsome woman emerged, dressed in white broadcloth and a hat with white lilacs; she carried a sunshade and walked with a free, energetic step, as if she were going out on a pleasant errand.

Mrs. Rosen darted quickly back into the house, lest her neighbor should hail her and stop to talk. She herself was in her kitchen housework dress, a crisp blue chambray which fitted smoothly over her tightly corseted figure, and her lustrous black hair was done in two smooth braids, wound flat at the back of her head, like a braided rug. She did not stop for a hat—her dark, ruddy, salmon-tinted skin had little to fear from the sun. She opened the half-closed oven door and took out a symmetrically plaited coffee-cake, beautifully browned, delicately peppered over with poppy seeds, with sugary margins about the twists. On the kitchen table a tray stood ready with cups and saucers. She wrapped the cake in a napkin, snatched up a little French coffee-pot with a black wooden handle, and ran across her green lawn, through the alley-way and the sandy, unkept yard next door, and entered her neighbor's house by the kitchen.

The kitchen was hot and empty, full of the untempered afternoon sun. A door stood open into the next room; a cluttered, hideous room, yet somehow homely. There, beside a goods-box covered with figured oilcloth, stood an old woman in a brown calico dress, washing her hot face and neck at a tin basin. She stood with her feet wide apart, in an attitude of profound weariness. She started guiltily as the visitor entered.

"Don't let me disturb you, Grandma," called Mrs. Rosen. "I always have my coffee at dis hour in the afternoon. I was just about to sit down to it when I thought: 'I will run over and see if Grandma Harris won't take a cup with me.' I hate to drink my coffee alone."

Grandma looked troubled,—at a loss. She folded her towel and concealed it behind a curtain hung across the corner of the room to make a poor sort of closet. The old lady was always composed in manner, but it was clear that she felt embarrassment.

"Thank you, Mrs. Rosen. What a pity Victoria just this minute went down town!"

"But dis time I came to see you yourself, Grandma. Don't let me disturb you. Sit down there in your own rocker, and I will put my tray on this little chair between us, so!"

Mrs. Harris sat down in her black wooden rocking-chair with curved arms and a faded cretonne pillow on the wooden seat. It stood in the corner beside a narrow spindle-frame lounge. She looked on silently while Mrs. Rosen uncovered the cake and delicately broke it with her plump, smooth, dusky-red hands. The old lady did not seem pleased,— seemed uncertain and apprehensive, indeed. But she was not fussy or fidgety. She had the kind of quiet, intensely quiet, dignity that comes from complete resignation to the chances of life. She watched Mrs. Rosen's deft hands out of grave, steady brown eyes.

"Dis is Mr. Rosen's favorite coffee-cake, Grandma, and I want you to try it. You are such a good cook yourself, I would like your opinion of my cake."

"It's very nice, ma'am," said Mrs. Harris politely, but without enthusiasm.

"And you aren't drinking your coffee; do you like more cream in it?"

"No, thank you. I'm letting it cool a little. I generally drink it that way."

"Of course she does," thought Mrs. Rosen, "since she never has her coffee until all the family are done breakfast!"

Mrs. Rosen had brought Grandma Harris coffee-cake time and again, but she knew that Grandma merely tasted it and saved it for her daughter Victoria, who was as fond of sweets as her own children, and jealous about them, moreover,—couldn't bear that special dainties should come into the house for anyone but herself. Mrs. Rosen, vexed at her failures, had determined that just once she would take a cake to "de old lady Harris," and with her own eyes see her eat it. The result was not at all she had hoped. Receiving a visitor alone, unsupervised by her daughter, having cake and coffee that should properly be saved for Victoria, was all so irregular that Mrs. Harris could not enjoy it. Mrs. Rosen doubted if she tasted the cake as she swallowed it,—certainly she ate it without relish, as a hollow form. But Mrs. Rosen enjoyed her own cake, at any rate, and she was glad, of an opportunity to sit quietly and look at Grandmother, who was more interesting to her than the handsome Victoria.

It was a queer place to be having coffee, when Mrs. Rosen liked order and comeliness so much: a hideous, cluttered room, furnished with a rocking-horse, a sewing-machine, an empty baby-buggy. A walnut table stood against a blind window, piled high with old magazines and tattered books, and children's caps and coats. There was a wash-stand (two wash-stands, if you counted the oilcloth-covered box as one). A corner of the room was curtained off with some black-and-red-striped cotton goods, for a clothes closet. In another corner was the wooden lounge with a thin mattress and a red calico spread which was Grandma's bed. Beside it was her wooden rocking-chair, and the little splint-bottom chair with the legs sawed short on which her darning-basket usually stood, but which Mrs. Rosen was now using for a tea-table.

The old lady was always impressive, Mrs. Rosen was thinking,—one could not say why. Perhaps it was the way she held her head,—so simply, unprotesting and unprotected; or the gravity of her large, deep-set brown eyes, a warm, reddish brown, though their look, always direct, seemed to ask nothing and hope for nothing. They were not cold, but inscrutable, with no kindling gleam of intercourse in them. There was the kind of nobility about her head that there is about an old lion's: an absence of self-consciousness, vanity, preoccupation—something absolute. Her grey hair was parted in the middle, wound in two little horns over her ears, and done in a little flat knot behind. Her mouth was large and composed,—resigned, the corners drooping. Mrs. Rosen had very seldom heard her laugh (and then it was a gentle, polite laugh which meant only politeness). But she had observed that whenever Mrs. Harris's grandchildren were about, tumbling all over her, asking for cookies, teasing her to read to them, the old lady looked happy.

As she drank her coffee, Mrs. Rosen tried one subject after another to engage Mrs. Harris's attention.

"Do you feel this hot weather, Grandma? I am afraid you are over the stove too much. Let those naughty children have a cold lunch occasionally."

"No'm, I don't mind the heat. It's apt to come on like this for a spell in May. I don't feel the stove. I'm accustomed to it."

"Oh, so am I! But I get very impatient with my cooking in hot weather. Do you miss your old home in Tennessee very much, Grandma?"

"No'm, I can't say I do. Mr. Templeton thought Colorado was a better place to bring up the children."

"But you had things much more comfortable down there, I'm sure. These little wooden houses are too hot in summer."

"Yes'm, we were more comfortable. We had more room."

"And a flower-garden, and beautiful old trees, Mrs. Templeton told me."

"Yes'm, we had a great deal of shade."

Mrs. Rosen felt that she was not getting anywhere. She almost believed that Grandma thought she had come on an equivocal errand, to spy out something in Victoria's absence. Well, perhaps she had! Just for once she would like to get past the others to the real grandmother,—and the real grandmother was on her guard, as always. At this moment she heard a faint miaow. Mrs. Harris rose, lifting herself by the wooden arms of her chair, said: "Excuse me," went into the kitchen, and opened the screen door.

In walked a large, handsome, thickly furred Maltese cat, with long whiskers and yellow eyes and a white star on his breast. He preceded Grandmother, waited until she sat down. Then he sprang up into her lap and settled himself comfortably in the folds of her full-gathered calico skirt. He rested his chin in his deep bluish fur and regarded Mrs. Rosen. It struck her that he held his head in just the way Grandmother held hers. And Grandmother now became more alive, as if some missing part of herself were restored.

"This is Blue Boy," she said, stroking him. "In winter, when the screen door ain't on, he lets himself in. He stands up on his hind legs and presses the thumb-latch with his paw, and just walks in like anybody."

"He's your cat, isn't he, Grandma?" Mrs. Rosen couldn't help prying just a little; if she could find but a single thing that was Grandma's own!

"He's our cat," replied Mrs. Harris. "We're all very fond of him. I expect he's Vickie's more'n anybody's."

"Of course!" groaned Mrs. Rosen to herself. "Dat Vickie is her mother over again."

Here Mrs. Harris made her first unsolicited remark. "If you was to be troubled with mice at any time, Mrs. Rosen, ask one of the boys to bring Blue Boy over to you, and he'll clear them out. He's a master mouser." She scratched the thick blue fur at the back of his neck, and he began a deep purring. Mrs. Harris smiled. "We call that spinning, back with us. Our children still say: 'Listen to the Blue Boy spin,' though none of 'em is ever heard a spinning-wheel—except maybe Vickie remembers."

"Did you have a spinning-wheel in your own house, Grandma Harris?"

"Yes'm. Miss Sadie Crummer used to come and spin for us. She was left with no home of her own, and it was to give her something to do, as much as anything, that we had her. I spun a good deal myself, in my young days." Grandmother stopped and put her hands on the arms of her chair, as if to rise. "Did you hear a door open? It might be Victoria."

"No, it was the wind shaking the screen door. Mrs. Templeton won't be home yet. She is probably in my husband's store this minute, ordering him about. All the merchants down town will take anything from your daughter. She is very popular wid de gentlemen, Grandma."

Mrs. Harris smiled complacently. "Yes'm. Victoria was always much admired."

At this moment a chorus of laughter broke in upon the warm silence, and a host of children, as it seemed to Mrs. Rosen, ran through the yard. The hand-pump on the back porch, outside the kitchen door, began to scrape and gurgle.

"It's the children, back from school," said Grandma. "They are getting a cool drink."

"But where is the baby, Grandma?"

"Vickie took Hughie in his cart over to Mr. Holliday's yard, where she studies. She's right good about minding him."

Mrs. Rosen was glad to hear that Vickie was good for something.

Three little boys came running in through the kitchen; the twins, aged ten, and Ronald, aged six, who went to kindergarten. They snatched off their caps and threw their jackets and school bags on the table, the sewing-machine, the rocking-horse.

"Howdy do, Mrs. Rosen." They spoke to her nicely. They had nice voices, nice faces, and were always courteous, like their father. "We are going to play in our back yard with some of the boys, Gram'ma," said one of the twins respectfully, and they ran out to join a troop of schoolmates who were already shouting and racing over that poor trampled back yard, strewn with velocipedes and croquet mallets and toy wagons, which was such an eyesore to Mrs. Rosen.

Mrs. Rosen got up and took her tray.

"Can't you stay a little, ma'am? Victoria will be here any minute."

But her tone let Mrs. Rosen know that Grandma really wished her to leave before Victoria returned.

A few moments after Mrs. Rosen had put the tray down in her own kitchen, Victoria Templeton came up the wooden sidewalk, attended by Mr. Rosen, who had quitted his store half a hour earlier than usual for the pleasure of walking home with her. Mrs. Templeton stopped by the picket fence to smile at the children playing in the back yard,—and it was a real smile, she was glad to see them. She called Ronald over to the fence to give him a kiss. He was hot and sticky.

"Was your teacher nice today? Now run in and ask Grandma to wash your face and put a clean waist on you."

II

That night Mrs. Harris got supper with an effort—had to drive herself harder than usual. Mandy, the bound girl they had brought with them from the South, noticed that the old lady was uncertain and short of breath. The hours from two to four, when Mrs. Harris usually rested, had not been at all restful this afternoon. There was an understood rule that Grandmother was not to receive visitors alone. Mrs. Rosen's call, and her cake and coffee, were too much out of the accepted order. Nervousness had prevented the old lady from getting any repose during her visit.

After the rest of the family had left the supper table, she went into the dining-room and took her place, but she ate very little. She put away the food that was left, and then, while Mandy washed the dishes, Grandma sat down in her rocking-chair in the dark and dozed.

The three little boys came in from playing under the electric light (arc lights had been but lately installed in Skyline) and began begging Mrs. Harris to read *Tom Sawyer* to them. Grandmother loved to read, anything at all, the Bible or the continued story in the Chicago weekly paper. She roused herself, lit her brass "safety lamp," and pulled her black rocker out of its corner to the wash-stand (the table was too far away from her corner, and anyhow it was completely covered with coats and school satchels). She put on her old-fashioned silver-rimmed spectacles and began to read. Ronald lay down on Grandmother's lounge bed, and the twins, Albert and Adelbert, called Bert and Del, sat down against the wall, one on a low box covered with felt, and the other on the little sawed-off chair upon which Mrs. Rosen had served coffee. They looked intently at Mrs. Harris, and she looked intently at the book.

Presently Vickie, the oldest grandchild, came in. She was fifteen. Her mother was entertaining callers in the parlor, callers who didn't interest Vickie, so she was on her way up to her own room by the kitchen stairway.

Mrs. Harris looked up over her glasses. "Vickie, maybe you'd take the book awhile, and I can do my darning."

"All right," said Vickie. Reading aloud was one of the things she would always do toward the general comfort. She sat down by the wash-stand and went on with the story. Grandmother got her darning-basket and began to drive her needle across great knee-holes in the boys' stockings. Sometimes she nodded for a moment, and her hands fell into her lap. After a while the little boy on the lounge went to sleep. But the twins sat upright, their hands on their knees, their round brown eyes fastened upon Vickie, and when there was anything funny, they giggled. They were chubby, dark-skinned little boys, with round jolly faces, white teeth, and yellow-brown eyes that were always bubbling with fun unless they were sad,—even then their eyes never got red or weepy. Their tears sparkled and fell; left no trace but a streak on the cheeks, perhaps.

Presently old Mrs. Harris gave out a long snore of utter defeat. She had been overcome at last. Vickie put down the book. "That's enough for tonight. Grandmother's sleepy, and Ronald's fast asleep. What'll we do with him?"

"Bert and me'll get him undressed," said Adelbert. The twins roused the sleepy little boy and prodded him up the back stairway to the bare room without window blinds, where he was put into his cot beside their double bed. Vickie's room was across the narrow hall-way; not much bigger than a closet, but, anyway, it was her own. She had a chair and an old dresser, and beside her bed was a high stool which she used as a lamp-table,—she always read in bed.

After Vickie went upstairs, the house was quiet. Hughie, the baby, was asleep in his mother's room, and Victoria herself, who still treated her husband as if he were her "beau," had persuaded him to take her down town to the ice-cream parlor. Grandmother's room, between the kitchen and the dining-room, was rather like a passageway; but now that the children were upstairs and Victoria was off enjoying herself somewhere, Mrs. Harris could be sure of enough privacy to undress. She took off the calico cover from her lounge bed and folded it up, put on her nightgown and white nightcap.

Mandy, the bound girl, appeared at the kitchen door.

"Miz' Harris," she said in a guarded tone, ducking her head, "you want me to rub your feet for you?"

For the first time in the long day the old woman's low composure broke a little. "Oh, Mandy, I would take it kindly of you!" she breathed gratefully.

That had to be done in the kitchen; Victoria didn't like anybody slopping about. Mrs. Harris put on an old checked shawl round her shoulders and followed Mandy. Beside the kitchen stove Mandy had a little wooden tub full of warm water. She knelt down and untied Mrs. Harris's garter strings and took off her flat cloth slippers and stockings.

"Oh, Miz' Harris, your feet an' legs is swelled turrible tonight!"

"I expect they air, Mandy. They feel like it."

"Pore soul!" murmured Mandy. She put Grandma's feet in the tub and, crouching beside it, slowly, slowly rubbed her swollen legs. Mandy was tired, too. Mrs. Harris sat in her nightcap and shawl, her hands crossed in her lap. She never asked for this greatest solace of the day; it was something that Mandy gave, who had nothing else to give. If there could be a comparison in absolutes, Mandy was the needier of the two,—but she was younger. The kitchen was quiet and full of shadow, with only the light from an old lantern. Neither spoke. Mrs. Harris dozed from comfort, and Mandy herself was half asleep as she performed one of the oldest rites of compassion.

Although Mrs. Harris's lounge had no springs, only a thin cotton mattress between her and the wooden slats, she usually went to sleep as soon as she was in bed. To be off her feet, to lie flat, to say over the psalm beginning: "*The Lord is my shepherd,*" was comfort enough. About four o'clock in the morning, however, she would begin to feel the hard slats under her, and the heaviness of the old home-made quilts, with weight but little warmth, on top of her. Then she would reach under her pillow for her little comforter (she called it that to herself) that Mrs. Rosen had given her. It was a tan sweater of very soft brushed wool, with one sleeve torn and ragged. A young nephew from Chicago had spent a fortnight with Mrs. Rosen last summer and had left this behind him. One morning, when Mrs. Harris went out to the stable at the back of the yard to pat Buttercup, the cow, Mrs. Rosen ran across the alley-way.

"Grandma Harris," she said, coming into the shelter of the stable, "I wonder if you could make any use of this sweater Sammy left? The yarn might be good for your darning."

Mrs. Harris felt of the article gravely. Mrs. Rosen thought her face brightened. "Yes'm, indeed I could use it. I thank you kindly."

She slipped it under her apron, carried it into the house with her, and concealed it under her mattress. There she had kept it ever since. She knew Mrs. Rosen understood how it was; that Victoria couldn't bear to have anything come into the house that was not for her to dispose of.

On winter nights, and even on summer nights after the cocks began to crow, Mrs. Harris often felt cold and lonely about the chest. Sometimes her cat, Blue Boy, would creep in beside her and warm that aching spot. But on spring and summer nights he was likely to be abroad skylarking, and this little sweater had become the dearest of Grandmother's few possessions. It was kinder to her, she used to think, as she wrapped it about her middle, than any of her own children had been. She had married at eighteen and had had eight children; but some died, and some were, as she said, scattered.

After she was warm in that tender spot under the ribs, the old woman could lie patiently on the slats, waiting for daybreak; thinking about the comfortable rambling old house in Tennessee, its feather beds and hand-woven rag carpets and splint-bottom chairs, the mahogany sideboard, and the marble-top parlor table; all that she had left behind to follow Victoria's fortunes.

She did not regret her decision; indeed, there had been no decision. Victoria had never once thought it possible that Ma should not go wherever she and the children went, and Mrs. Harris had never thought it possible. Of course she regretted Tennessee, though she would never admit it to Mrs. Rosen:—the old neighbors, the yard and garden she had worked in all her life, the apple trees she had planted, the lilac arbor, tall enough to walk in, which she had clipped and shaped so many years. Especially she missed her lemon tree, in a tub on the front porch, which bore little lemons almost every summer, and folks would come for miles to see it.

But the road had led westward, and Mrs. Harris didn't believe that women, especially old women, could say when or where they would stop. They were tied to the chariot of young life, and had to go where it went, because they were needed. Mrs. Harris had gathered from Mrs. Rosen's manner, and from comments she occasionally dropped, that the Jewish people had an altogether different attitude toward their old folks; therefore her friendship with this kind neighbor was almost as disturbing as it was pleasant. She didn't want Mrs. Rosen to think that she was "put upon," that there was anything unusual or pitiful in her lot. To be pitied was the deepest hurt anybody could know. And if Victoria once suspected Mrs. Rosen's indignation, it would be all over. She would freeze her neighbor out, and that friendly voice, that quick pleasant chatter with the little foreign twist, would thenceforth be heard only at a distance, in the alleyway or across the fence. Victoria had a good heart, but she was terribly proud and could not bear the least criticism.

As soon as the grey light began to steal into the room, Mrs. Harris would get up softly and wash at the basin on the oilcloth-covered box. She would wet her hair above her forehead, comb it over with a little bone comb set in a tin rim, do it up in two smooth little horns over her ears, wipe the comb dry, and put it away in the pocket of her full-gathered calico skirt. She left nothing lying about. As soon as she was dressed, she made her bed, folding her nightgown and nightcap under the pillow, the sweater under the mattress. She smoothed the heavy quilts, and drew the red calico spread neatly over all. Her towel was hung on its special nail behind the curtain. Her soap she kept in a tin tobacco-box; the children's soap was in a crockery saucer. If her soap or towel got mixed up with the children's, Victoria was always sharp about it. The little rented house was much too small for the family, and Mrs. Harris and her "things" were almost required to be invisible. Two clean calico dresses hung in the curtained corner; another was on her back, and a fourth was in the wash. Behind the curtain there was always a good supply of aprons; Victoria bought them at church fairs, and it was a great satisfaction to Mrs. Harris to put on a clean one whenever she liked. Upstairs, in Mandy's attic room over the kitchen, hung a black cashmere dress and a black bonnet with a long crêpe veil, for the rare occasions when Mr. Templeton hired a double buggy and horses and drove the family to a picnic or to Decoration Day exercises. Mrs. Harris rather dreaded these drives, for Victoria was usually cross afterward.

When Mrs. Harris went out into the kitchen to get breakfast, Mandy always had the fire started and the water boiling. They enjoyed a quiet half-hour before the little boys came running down the stairs, always in a good humor. In winter the boys had their breakfast in the kitchen, with Vickie. Mrs. Harris made Mandy eat the cakes and fried ham the children left, so that she would not fast so long. Mr. and Mrs. Templeton breakfasted rather late, in the dining-room, and they always had fruit and thick cream,—a small pitcher of the very thickest was for Mrs. Templeton. The children were never fussy about their food. As Grandmother often said feelingly to Mrs. Rosen, they were as little trouble as children could possibly be. They sometimes tore their clothes, of course, or got sick. But even when Albert had an abscess in his ear and was in such pain, he would lie for hours on Grandmother's lounge with his cheek on a bag of hot salt, if only she or Vickie would read aloud to him.

"It's true, too, what de old lady says," remarked Mrs. Rosen to her husband one night at supper, "dey are nice children. No one ever taught them anything, but they have good instincts, even dat Vickie. And think, if you please, of all the self-sacrificing mothers we know,—Fannie and Esther, to come near home; how they have planned for those children from infancy and given them every advantage. And now ingratitude and coldness is what dey meet with."

Mr. Rosen smiled his teasing smile. "Evidently your sister and mine have the wrong method. The way to make your children unselfish is to be comfortably selfish yourself."

"But dat woman takes no more responsibility for her children than a cat takes for her kittens. Nor does poor young Mr. Templeton, for dat matter. How can he expect to get so many children started in life, I ask you? It is not at all fair!"

Mr. Rosen sometimes had to hear altogether too much about the Templetons, but he was patient, because it was a bitter sorrow to Mrs. Rosen that she had no children. There was nothing else in the world she wanted so much.

III

Mrs. Rosen in one of her blue working dresses, the indigo blue that became a dark skin and dusky red cheeks with a tone of salmon color, was in her shining kitchen, washing her beautiful dishes—her neighbors often wondered why she used her best china and linen every day—when Vickie Templeton came in with a book under her arm.

"Good day, Mrs. Rosen. Can I have the second volume?"

"Certainly. You know where the books are." She spoke coolly, for it always annoyed her that Vickie never suggested wiping the dishes or helping with such household work as happened to be going on when she dropped in. She hated the girl's bringing-up so much that sometimes she almost hated the girl.

Vickie strolled carelessly through the dining-room into the parlor and opened the doors of one of the big bookcases. Mr. Rosen had a large library, and a great many unusual books. There was a complete set of the Waverley Novels in German, for example; thick, dumpy little volumes bound in tooled leather, with very black type and dramatic engravings printed on wrinkled, yellowing pages. There were many French books, and some of the German classics done into English, such as Coleridge's translation of Schiller's *Wallenstein*.

Of course no other house in Skyline was in the least like Mrs. Rosen's; it was the nearest thing to an art gallery and a museum that the Templetons had ever seen. All the rooms were carpeted alike (that was very unusual), with a soft velvet carpet, little blue and rose flowers scattered on a rose-grey ground. The deep chairs were upholstered in dark blue velvet. The walls were hung with engravings in pale gold frames: some of Raphael's "Hours," a large soft engraving of a castle on the Rhine, and another of cypress trees about a Roman ruin, under a full moon. There were a number of water-color sketches, made in Italy by Mr. Rosen himself when he was a boy. A rich uncle had taken him abroad as his secretary. Mr. Rosen was a reflective, unambitious man, who didn't mind keeping a clothing-store in a little Western town, so long as he had a great deal of time to read philosophy. He was the only unsuccessful member of a large, rich Jewish family.

Last August, when the heat was terrible in Skyline, and the crops were burned up on all the farms to the north, and the wind from the pink and yellow sand-hills to the south blew so hot that it singed the few green lawns in the town, Vickie had taken to dropping in upon Mrs. Rosen at the very hottest part of the afternoon. Mrs. Rosen knew, of course, that it was probably because the girl had no other cool and quiet place to go—her room at home under the roof would be hot enough! Now, Mrs. Rosen liked to undress and take a nap from three to five,—if only to get out of her tight corsets, for she would have an hour-glass figure at any cost. She told Vickie firmly that she was welcome to come if she would read in the parlor with the blind up only a little way, and would be still as a mouse. Vickie came, meekly enough, but she seldom read. She would take a sofa pillow and lie down on the soft carpet and look up at the pictures in the dusky room, and feel a happy, pleasant excitement from the heat and glare outside and the deep shadow and quiet within. Curiously enough, Mrs. Rosen's house never made her dissatisfied with her own; she thought that very nice, too.

Mrs. Rosen, leaving her kitchen in a state of such perfection as the Templetons were unable to sense or to admire, came into the parlor and found her visitor sitting cross-legged on the floor before one of the bookcases.

"Well, Vickie, and how did you get along with *Wilhelm Meister*?"

"I like it," said Vickie.

Mrs. Rosen shrugged. The Templetons always said that; quite as if a book or a cake were lucky to win their approbation.

"Well, *what* did you like?"

"I guess I liked all that about the theatre and Shakespeare best."

"It's rather celebrated," remarked Mrs. Rosen dryly. "And are you studying every day? Do you think you will be able to win that scholarship?"

"I don't know. I'm going to try awful hard."

Mrs. Rosen wondered whether any Templeton knew how to try very hard. She reached for her work-basket and began to do cross-stitch. It made her nervous to sit with folded hands. Vickie was looking at a German book in her lap, an illustrated edition of *Faust*. She had stopped at a very German picture of Gretchen entering the church, with Faustus gazing at her from behind a rose tree, Mephisto at his shoulder.

"I wish I could read this," she said, frowning at the black Gothic text. "It's splendid, isn't it?"

Mrs. Rosen rolled her eyes upward and sighed. "Oh, my dear, one of de world's masterpieces!"

That meant little to Vickie. She had not been taught to

respect masterpieces, she had no scale of that sort in her mind. She cared about a book only because it took hold of her.

She kept turning over the pages. Between the first and second parts, in this edition, there was inserted the *Dies Iræ* hymn in full. She stopped and puzzled over it for a long while.

"Here is something I can read," she said, showing the page to Mrs. Rosen.

Mrs. Rosen looked up from her cross-stitch. "There you have the advantage of me. I do not read Latin. You might translate it for me."

Vickie began:

"Day of wrath, upon that day
The world to ashes melts away,
As David and the Sibyl say.

"But that don't give you the rhyme; every line ought to end in two syllables."

"Never mind if it doesn't give the meter," corrected Mrs. Rosen kindly; "go on, if you can."

Vickie went on stumbling through the Latin verses, and Mrs. Rosen sat watching her. You couldn't tell about Vickie. She wasn't pretty, yet Mrs. Rosen found her attractive. She liked her sturdy build and the steady vitality that glowed in her rosy skin and dark blue eyes,—even gave a springy quality to her curly reddish-brown hair, which she still wore in a single braid down her back. Mrs. Rosen liked to have Vickie about because she was never listless or dreamy or apathetic.

A half-smile nearly always played about her lips and eyes, and it was there because she was pleased with something, not because she wanted to be agreeable. Even a half-smile made her cheeks dimple. She had what her mother called "a happy disposition."

When she finished the verses, Mrs. Rosen nodded approvingly. "Thank you, Vickie. The very next time I go to Chicago, I will try to get an English translation of *Faust* for you."

"But I want to read this one." Vickie's open smile darkened. "What I want is to pick up any of these books and just read them, like you and Mr. Rosen do."

The dusky red of Mrs. Rosen's cheeks grew a trifle deeper. Vickie never paid compliments, absolutely never; but if she really admired anyone, something in her voice betrayed it so convincingly that one felt flattered. When she dropped a remark of this kind, she added another link to the chain of responsibility which Mrs. Rosen unwillingly bore and tried to shake off—the irritating sense of being somehow responsible for Vickie, since, God knew, no one else felt responsible.

Once or twice, when she happened to meet pleasant young Mr. Templeton alone, she had tried to talk to him seriously about his daughter's future. "She has finished de school here, and she should be getting training of some sort; she is growing up," she told him severely.

He laughed and said in his way that was so honest, and so disarmingly sweet and frank: "Oh, don't remind me, Mrs.

Rosen! I just pretend to myself she isn't. I want to keep my little daughter as long as I can." And there it ended.

Sometimes Vickie Templeton seemed so dense, so utterly unperceptive, that Mrs. Rosen was ready to wash her hands of her. Then some queer streak of sensibility in the child would make her change her mind. Last winter, when Mrs. Rosen came home from a visit to her sister in Chicago, she brought with her a new cloak of the sleeveless dolman type, black velvet, lined with grey and white squirrel skins, a grey skin next a white. Vickie, so indifferent to clothes, fell in love with that cloak. Her eyes followed it with delight whenever Mrs. Rosen wore it. She found it picturesque, romantic. Mrs. Rosen had been captivated by the same thing in the cloak, and had bought it with a shrug, knowing it would be quite out of place in Skyline; and Mr. Rosen, when she first produced it from her trunk, had laughed and said; "Where did you get that?—out of *Rigoletto*?" It looked like that—but how could Vickie know?

Vickie's whole family puzzled Mrs. Rosen; their feelings were so much finer than their way of living. She bought milk from the Templetons because they kept a cow—which Mandy milked,—and every night one of the twins brought the milk to her in a tin pail. Whichever boy brought it, she always called him Albert—she thought Adelbert a silly, Southern name.

One night when she was fitting the lid on an empty pail, she said severely:

"Now, Albert, I have put some cookies for Grandma in

this pail, wrapped in a napkin. And they are for Grandma, remember, not for your mother or Vickie."

"Yes'm."

When she turned to him to give him the pail, she saw two full crystal globes in the little boy's eyes, just ready to break. She watched him go softly down the path and dash those tears away with the back of his hand. She was sorry. She hadn't thought the little boys realized that their household was somehow a queer one.

Queer or not, Mrs. Rosen liked to go there better than to most houses in the town. There was something easy, cordial, and carefree in the parlor that never smelled of being shut up, and the ugly furniture looked hospitable. One felt a pleasantness in the human relationships. These people didn't seem to know there were such things as struggle or exactness or competition in the world. They were always genuinely glad to see you, had time to see you, and were usually gay in mood—all but Grandmother, who had the kind of gravity that people who take thought of human destiny must have. But even she liked light-heartedness in others; she drudged, indeed, to keep it going.

There were houses that were better kept, certainly, but the housekeepers had no charm, no gentleness of manner, were like hard little machines, most of them; and some were grasping and narrow. The Templetons were not selfish or scheming. Anyone could take advantage of them, and many people did. Victoria might eat all the cookies her neighbor sent in, but she would give away anything she had. She was always ready to lend her dresses and hats and bits of jewelry for the school theatricals, and she never worked people for favors.

As for Mr. Templeton (people usually called him "young Mr. Templeton"), he was too delicate to collect his just debts. His boyish, eager-to-please manner, his fair complexion and blue eyes and young face, made him seem very soft to some of the hard old money-grubbers on Main Street, and the fact that he always said "Yes, sir," and "No, sir," to men older than himself furnished a good deal of amusement to by-standers.

Two years ago, when this Templeton family came to Skyline and moved into the house next door, Mrs. Rosen was inconsolable. The new neighbors had a lot of children, who would always be making a racket. They put a cow and a horse into the empty barn, which would mean dirt and flies. They strewed their back yard with packing-cases and did not pick them up.

She first met Mrs. Templeton at an afternoon card party, in a house at the extreme north end of the town, fully half a mile away, and she had to admit that her new neighbor was an attractive woman, and that there was something warm and genuine about her. She wasn't in the least willowy or languishing, as Mrs. Rosen had usually found Southern ladies to be. She was high-spirited and direct; a trifle imperious, but with a shade of diffidence, too, as if she was trying to adjust herself to a new group of people and to do the right thing.

While they were at the party, a blinding snowstorm came on, with a hard wind. Since they lived next door to each other, Mrs. Rosen and Mrs. Templeton struggled homeward together through the blizzard. Mrs. Templeton seemed delighted with the rough weather; she laughed like a big country girl whenever she made a mis-step off the obliterated sidewalk and sank up to her knees in a snow-drift.

"Take care, Mrs. Rosen," she kept calling, "keep to the right! Don't spoil your nice coat. My, ain't this real winter? We never had it like this back with us."

When they reached the Templeton's gate, Victoria wouldn't hear of Mrs. Rosen's going farther. "No, indeed, Mrs. Rosen, you come right in with me and get dry, and Ma'll make you a hot toddy while I take the baby."

By this time Mrs. Rosen had begun to like her neighbor, so she went in. To her surprise, the parlor was neat and comfortable—the children did not strew things about there, apparently. The hard-coal burner threw out a warm red glow. A faded, respectable Brussels carpet covered the floor, an old-fashioned wooden clock ticked on the walnut bookcase. There were a few easy chairs, and no hideous ornaments about. She rather liked the old oil-chromos on the wall: "Hagar and Ishmael in the Wilderness," and "The Light of the World." While Mrs. Rosen dried her feet on the nickel base of the stove, Mrs. Templeton excused herself and withdrew to the next room,—her bedroom,—took off her silk dress and corsets, and put on a white challis negligee. She reappeared with the baby, who was not crying, exactly, but making eager, passionate, gasping entreaties,—faster and faster, tenser and tenser, as he felt his dinner nearer and nearer and yet not his.

Mrs. Templeton sat down in a low rocker by the stove and began to nurse him, holding him snugly but carelessly, still talking to Mrs. Rosen about the card party, and laughing about their wade home through the snow. Hughie, the baby, fell to work so fiercely that beads of sweat came out all over his flushed forehead. Mrs. Rosen could not help admiring him and his mother. They were so comfortable and complete. When he was changed to the other side, Hughie resented the interruption a little; but after a time he became soft and bland, as smooth as oil, indeed; began looking about him as he drew in his milk. He finally dropped the nipple from his lips altogether, turned on his mother's arm, and looked inquiringly at Mrs. Rosen.

"What a beautiful baby!" she exclaimed from her heart. And he was. A sort of golden baby. His hair was like sunshine, and his long lashes were gold over such gay blue eyes. There seemed to be a gold glow in his soft pink skin, and he had the smile of a cherub.

"We think he's a pretty boy," said Mrs. Templeton. "He's the prettiest of my babies. Though the twins were mighty cunning little fellows. I hated the idea of twins, but the minute I saw them, I couldn't resist them."

Just then old Mrs. Harris came in, walking widely in her full-gathered skirt and felt-soled shoes, bearing a tray with two smoking goblets upon it.

"This is my mother, Mrs. Harris, Mrs. Rosen," said Mrs. Templeton.

"I'm glad to know you, ma'am," said Mrs. Harris. "Victoria, let me take the baby, while you two ladies have your toddy."

"Oh, don't take him away, Mrs. Harris, please!" cried Mrs. Rosen.

The old lady smiled. "I won't. I'll set right here. He never frets with his grandma."

When Mrs. Rosen had finished her excellent drink she asked if she might hold the baby, and Mrs. Harris placed him on her lap. He made a few rapid boxing motions with his two fists, then braced himself on his heels and the back of his head, and lifted himself up in an arc. When he dropped back, he looked up at Mrs. Rosen with his most intimate smile. "See what a smart boy I am!"

When Mrs. Rosen walked home, feeling her way through the snow by following the fence, she knew she could never stay away from a house where there was a baby like that one.

IV

Vickie did her studying in a hammock hung between two tall cottonwood trees over in the Roadmaster's green yard. The Roadmaster had the finest yard in Skyline, on the edge of the town, just where the sandy plain and the sage-brush began. His family went back to Ohio every summer, and Bert and Del Templeton were paid to take care of his lawn, to turn the sprinkler on at the right hours and to cut the grass. They were really too little to run the heavy lawn-mower very well, but they were able to manage because they were twins. Each took one end of the handle-bar, and they pushed together like a pair of fat Shetland ponies. They were very proud of being able to keep the lawn so nice, and worked hard on it. They cut Mrs. Rosen's grass once a week, too, and did it so well that she wondered why in the world they never did anything about their own yard. They didn't have city water, to be sure (it was expensive), but she thought they might pick up a few velocipedes and iron hoops, and dig up the messy "flower-bed," that was even uglier than the naked gravel spots. She was particularly offended by a deep ragged ditch, a miniature arroyo, which ran across the back yard, serving no purpose and looking very dreary.

One morning she said craftily to the twins, when she was paying them for cutting her grass:

"And, boys, why don't you just shovel the sand-pile by your fence into dat ditch, and make your back yard smooth?"

"Oh, no, ma'am," said Adelbert with feeling. "We like to have the ditch to build bridges over!"

Ever since vacation began, the twins had been busy getting the Roadmaster's yard ready for the Methodist lawn party. When Mrs. Holliday, the Roadmaster's wife, went away for the summer, she always left a key with the Ladies' Aid Society and invited them to give their ice-cream social at her place.

This year the date set for the party was June fifteenth. The day was a particularly fine one, and as Mr. Holliday himself had been called to Cheyenne on railroad business, the twins felt personally responsible for everything. They got out to the Holliday place early in the morning, and stayed on guard all day. Before noon the drayman brought a wagonload of card-tables and folding chairs, which the boys placed in chosen spots under the cottonwood trees. In the afternoon the Methodist ladies arrived and opened up the kitchen to receive the freezers of home-made ice-cream, and the cakes which the congregation donated. Indeed, all the good cake-bakers in town were expected to send a cake. Grandma Harris baked a white cake, thickly iced and covered with freshly grated coconut, and Vickie took it over in the afternoon.

Mr. and Mrs. Rosen, because they belonged to no church, contributed to the support of all, and usually went to the church suppers in winter and the socials in summer. On this warm June evening they set out early, in order to take a walk first. They strolled along the hard graveled road that led out through the sage toward the sand-hills; tonight it led toward the moon, just rising over the sweep of dunes. The sky was almost as blue as at midday, and had that look of being very near and very soft which it has in desert countries. The moon, too, looked very near, soft and bland and innocent. Mrs. Rosen admitted that in the Adirondacks, for which she was always secretly homesick in summer, the moon had a much colder brilliance, seemed farther off and made of a harder metal. This moon gave the sage-brush plain and the drifted sand-hills the softness of velvet. All countries were beautiful to Mr. Rosen. He carried a country of his own in his mind, and was able to unfold it like a tent in any wilderness.

When they at last turned back toward the town, they saw groups of people, women in white dresses, walking toward the dark spot where the paper lanterns made a yellow light underneath the cottonwoods. High above, the rustling tree-tops stirred free in the flood of moonlight.

The lighted yard was surrounded by a low board fence, painted the dark red Burlington color, and as the Rosens drew near, they noticed four children standing close together in the shadow of some tall elder bushes just outside the fence. They were the poor Maude children; their mother was the washwoman, the Rosens' laundress and the Templetons'. People said that every one of those children had a different father. But good laundresses were few, and even the members of the Ladies' Aid were glad to get Mrs. Maude's services at a dollar a day, though they didn't like their children to play with hers. Just as the Rosens approached, Mrs. Templeton came out from the lighted square, leaned over the fence, and addressed the little Maudes.

"I expect you children forgot your dimes, now didn't you? Never mind, here's a dime for each of you, so come along and have your ice-cream."

The Maudes put out small hands and said: "Thank you," but not one of them moved.

"Come along, Francie" (the oldest girl was named Frances). "Climb right over the fence." Mrs. Templeton reached over and gave her a hand, and the little boys quickly scrambled after their sister. Mrs. Templeton took them to a table which Vickie and the twins had just selected as being especially private—they liked to do things together.

"Here, Vickie, let the Maudes sit at your table, and take care they get plenty of cake."

The Rosens had followed close behind Mrs. Templeton, and Mr. Rosen now overtook her and said in his most courteous and friendly manner: "Good evening, Mrs. Templeton. Will you have ice-cream with us?" He always used the local idioms, though his voice and enunciation made them sound altogether different from Skyline speech.

"Indeed I will, Mr. Rosen. Mr. Templeton will be late. He went out to his farm yesterday, and I don't know just when to expect him."

Vickie and the twins were disappointed at not having their table to themselves, when they had come early and found a nice one; but they knew it was right to look out for the dreary little Maudes, so they moved close together and made room for them. The Maudes didn't cramp them long. When the three boys had eaten the last crumb of cake and licked their spoons, Francie got up and led them to a green slope by the fence, just outside the lighted circle. "Now set down, and watch and see how folks do," she told them. The boys looked to Francie for commands and support. She was really Amos Maude's child, born before he ran away to the Klondike, and it had been rubbed into them that this made a difference.

The Templeton children made their ice-cream linger out, and sat watching the crowd. They were glad to see their mother go to Mr. Rosen's table, and noticed how nicely he placed a chair for her and insisted upon putting a scarf about her shoulders. Their mother was wearing her new dotted Swiss, with many ruffles, all edged with black ribbon, and wide ruffly sleeves. As the twins watched her over their spoons, they thought how much prettier their mother was than any of the other women, and how becoming her new dress was. The children got as much satisfaction as Mrs. Harris out of Victoria's good looks.

Mr. Rosen was well pleased with Mrs. Templeton and her new dress, and with her kindness to the little Maudes. He thought her manner with them just right,—warm, spontaneous, without anything patronizing. He always admired her way with her own children, though Mrs. Rosen thought it too casual. Being a good mother, he believed, was much more a matter of physical poise and richness than of sentimentalizing and reading doctor-books. Tonight he was more talkative than usual, and in his quiet way made Mrs. Templeton feel his real friendliness and admiration. Unfortunately, he made other people feel it, too.

Mrs. Jackson, a neighbor who didn't like the Templetons, had been keeping an eye on Mr. Rosen's table. She was a stout square woman of imperturbable calm, effective in regulating the affairs of the community because she never lost her temper, and could say the most cutting things in calm, even kindly, tones. Her face was smooth and placid as a mask, rather good-humored, and the fact that one eye had a cast and looked askance made it the more difficult to see through her intentions. When she had been lingering about the Rosens' table for some time, studying Mr. Rosen's pleasant attentions to Mrs. Templeton, she brought up a trayful of cake.

"You folks are about ready for another helping," she remarked affably.

Mrs. Rosen spoke. "I want some of Grandma Harris's cake. It's a white coconut, Mrs. Jackson."

"How about you, Mrs. Templeton, would you like some of your own cake?"

"Indeed I would," said Mrs. Templeton heartily. "Ma said she had good luck with it. I didn't see it. Vickie brought it over."

Mrs. Jackson deliberately separated the slices on her tray with two forks. "Well," she remarked with a chuckle that really sounded amiable, "I don't know but I'd like my cakes, if I kept somebody in the kitchen to bake them for me."

Mr. Rosen for once spoke quickly. "If I had a cook like Grandma Harris in my kitchen, I'd live in it!" he declared.

Mrs. Jackson smiled. "I don't know as we feel like that, Mrs. Templeton? I tell Mr. Jackson that my idea of coming up in the world would be to forget I had a cook-stove, like Mrs. Templeton. But we can't all be lucky."

Mr. Rosen could not tell how much was malice and how much was stupidity. What he chiefly detected was self-satisfaction; the craftiness of the coarse-fibered country girl putting catch questions to the teacher. Yes, he decided, the woman was merely showing off—she regarded it as an accomplishment to make people uncomfortable.

Mrs. Templeton didn't at once take it in. Her training was all to the end that you must give a guest everything you have, even if he happens to be your worst enemy, and that to cause anyone embarrassment is a frightful and humiliating blunder. She felt hurt without knowing just why, but all evening it kept growing clearer to her that this was another of those thrusts from the outside which she couldn't understand. The neighbors were sure to take sides against her, apparently, if they came often to see her mother.

Mr. Rosen tried to distract Mrs. Templeton but he could feel the poison working. On the way home the children knew something had displeased or hurt their mother. When they went into the house, she told them to go upstairs at once, as she had a headache. She was severe and distant. When Mrs. Harris suggested making her some peppermint tea, Victoria threw up her chin.

"I don't want anybody waiting on me. I just want to be let alone." And she withdrew without saying good-night, or "Are you all right, Ma?" as she usually did.

Left alone, Mrs. Harris sighed and began to turn down her bed. She knew, as well as if she had been at the social, what kind of thing had happened. Some of those prying ladies of the Woman's Relief Corps, or the Woman's Christian Temperance Union, had been intimating to Victoria that her mother was "put upon." Nothing ever made Victoria cross but criticism. She was jealous of small attentions paid to Mrs. Harris, because she felt they were paid "behind her back" or "over her head," in a way that implied reproach to her. Victoria had been a belle in their own town in Tennessee, but here she was not very popular, no matter how many pretty dresses she wore, and she couldn't bear it. She felt as if her mother and Mr. Templeton must be somehow to blame; at least they ought to protect her from whatever was disagreeable—they always had!

V

Mrs. Harris wakened at about four o'clock, as usual, before the house was stirring, and lay thinking about their position in this new town. She didn't know why the neighbors acted so; she was as much in the dark as Victoria. At home, back in Tennessee, her place in the family was not exceptional, but perfectly regular. Mrs. Harris had replied to Mrs. Rosen, when that lady asked why in the world she didn't break Vickie in to help her in the kitchen: "We are only young once, and trouble comes soon enough." Young girls, in the South, were supposed to be carefree and foolish; the fault Grandmother found in Vickie was that she wasn't foolish enough. When the foolish girl married and began to have children, everything else must give way to that. She must be humored and given the best of everything, because having children was hard on a woman, and it was the most impor-tant thing in the world. In Tennessee every young married woman in good circumstances had an older woman in the house, a mother or mother-in-law or an old aunt, who managed the household economies and directed the help.

That was the great difference; in Tennessee there had been plenty of helpers. There was old Miss Sadie Crummer, who came to the house to spin and sew and mend; old Mrs. Smith, who always arrived to help at butchering- and preserving-time; Lizzie, the colored girl, who did the washing and who ran in every day to help Mandy. There were plenty more, who came whenever one of Lizzie's bare-foot boys ran to fetch them. The hills were full of solitary old women, or women but slightly attached to some household, who were glad to come to Miz' Harris's for good food and a warm bed, and the little present that either Mrs. Harris or Victoria slipped into their carpet-sack when they went away.

To be sure, Mrs. Harris, and the other women of her age who managed their daughter's house, kept in the background; but it was their own background, and they ruled it jealously. They left the front porch and the parlor to the young married couple and their young friends; the old women spent most of their lives in the kitchen and pantries and back dining-room. But there they ordered life to their own taste, entertained their friends, dispensed charity, and heard the troubles of the poor. Moreover, back there it was Grandmother's own house they lived in. Mr. Templeton came of a superior family and had what Grandmother called "blood," but no property. He never so much as mended one of the steps to the front porch without consulting

Mrs. Harris. Even "back home," in the aristocracy, there were old women who went on living like young ones—gave parties and drove out in their carriage and "went North" in the summer. But among the middle-class people and the country-folk, when a woman was a widow and had married daughters, she considered herself an old woman and wore full-gathered black dresses and a black bonnet and became a housekeeper. She accepted this estate unprotestingly, almost gratefully.

The Templetons' troubles began when Mr. Templeton's aunt died and left him a few thousand dollars, and he got the idea of bettering himself. The twins were little then, and he told Mrs. Harris his boys would have a better chance in Colorado—everybody was going West. He went alone first, and got a good position with a mining company in the mountains of southern Colorado. He had been book-keeper in the bank in his home town, had "grown up in the bank," as they said. He was industrious and honorable, and the managers of the mining company liked him, even if they laughed at his polite, soft-spoken manners. He could have held his position indefinitely, and maybe got a promotion. But the altitude of that mountain town was too high for his family. All the children were sick there; Mrs. Templeton was ill most of the time and nearly died when Ronald was born. Hillary Templeton lost his courage and came north to the flat, sunny, semi-arid country between Wray and Cheyenne, to work for an irrigation project. So far, things had not gone well with him. The pinch told on everyone, but most on

Grandmother. Here, in Skyline, she had all her accustomed responsibilities, and no helper but Mandy. Mrs. Harris was no longer living in a feudal society, where there were plenty of landless people, glad to render service to the more fortunate, but in a snappy little Western democracy, where every man was as good as his neighbor and out to prove it.

Neither Mrs. Harris nor Mrs. Templeton understood just what was the matter; they were hurt and dazed, merely. Victoria knew that here she was censured and criticized, she who had always been so admired and envied! Grandmother knew that these meddlesome "Northerners" said things that made Victoria suspicious and unlike herself; made her unwilling that Mrs. Harris should receive visitors alone, or accept marks of attention that seemed offered in compassion for her state.

These women who belonged to clubs and Relief Corps lived differently, Mrs. Harris knew, but she herself didn't like the way they lived. She believed that somebody ought to be in the parlor, and somebody in the kitchen. She wouldn't for the world have had Victoria go about every morning in a short gingham dress, with bare arms, and a dust-cap on her head to hide the curling-kids, as these brisk housekeepers did. To Mrs. Harris that would have meant real poverty, coming down in the world so far that one could no longer keep up appearances. Her life was hard now, to be sure, since the family went on increasing and Mr. Templeton's means went on decreasing; but she certainly valued respectability above personal comfort, and she could go on a good way yet if they always had a cool pleasant parlor, with Victoria

properly dressed to receive visitors. To keep Victoria different from these "ordinary" women meant everything to Mrs.
Harris. She realized that Mrs. Rosen managed to be mistress
of any situation, either in kitchen or parlor, but that was
because she was "foreign." Grandmother perfectly understood that their neighbor had a superior cultivation which
made everything she did an exercise of skill. She knew well
enough that their own ways of cooking and cleaning were
primitive beside Mrs. Rosen's.

If only Mr. Templeton's business affairs would look up,
they could rent a larger house, and everything would be
better. They might even get a German girl to come in and
help—but now there was no place to put her. Grandmother's
own lot could improve only with the family fortunes—any
comfort for herself, aside from that of the family, was incon-
ceivable to her; and on the other hand she could have no real
unhappiness while the children were well, and good, and
fond of her and their mother. That was why it was worth
while to get up early in the morning and make her bed neat
and draw the red spread smooth. The little boys loved to lie
on her lounge and her pillows when they were tired. When
they were sick, Ronald and Hughie wanted to be in her lap.
They had no physical shrinking from her because she was
old. And Victoria was never jealous of the children's want-
ing to be with her so much; that was a mercy!

Sometimes, in the morning, if her feet ached more than
usual, Mrs. Harris felt a little low. (Nobody did anything about
broken arches in those days, and the common endurance test

of old age was to keep going after every step cost something.) She would hang up her towel with a sigh and go into the kitchen, feeling that it was hard to make a start. But the moment she heard the children running down the uncarpeted back stairs, she forgot to be low. Indeed, she ceased to be an individual, an old woman with aching feet; she became part of a group, became a relationship. She was drunk up into their freshness when they burst in upon her, telling her about their dreams, explaining their troubles with buttons and shoe-laces and underwear shrunk too small. The tired, solitary old woman Grandmother had been at daybreak vanished; suddenly the morning seemed as important to her as it did to the children, and the morning ahead stretched out sunshiny, important.

VI

The day after the Methodist social, Blue Boy didn't come for his morning milk; he always had it in a clean saucer on the covered back porch, under the long bench where the tin wash-tubs stood ready for Mrs. Maude. After the children had finished breakfast, Mrs. Harris sent Mandy out to look for the cat.

The girl came back in a minute, her eyes big.

"Law me, Miz' Harris, he's awful sick. He's a-layin' in the straw in the barn. He's swallered a bone, or havin' a fit or somethin.'"

Grandmother threw an apron over her head and went out to see for herself. The children went with her. Blue Boy was retching and choking, and his yellow eyes were filled up with rheum.

"Oh, Gram'ma, what's the matter?" the boys cried.

"It's the distemper. How could he have got it?" Her voice was so harsh that Ronald began to cry. "Take Ronald back to the house, Del. He might get bit. I wish I'd kept my word and never had a cat again!"

"Why, Gram'ma!" Albert looked at her. "Won't Blue Boy get well?"

"Not from the distemper, he won't."

"But Gram'ma, can't I run for the veter'nary?"

"You gether up an armful of hay. We'll take him into the coal-house, where I can watch him."

Mrs. Harris waited until the spasm was over, then picked up the limp cat and carried him to the coal-shed that opened off the back porch. Albert piled the hay in one corner—the coal was low, since it was summer—and they spread a piece of old carpet on the hay and made a bed for Blue Boy. "Now you run along with Adelbert. There'll be a lot of work to do on Mr. Holliday's yard, cleaning up after the sociable. Mandy an' me'll watch Blue Boy. I expect he'll sleep for a while."

Albert went away regretfully, but the dray-man and some of the Methodist ladies were in Mr. Holliday's yard, packing chairs and tables and ice-cream freezers into the wagon, and the twins forgot the sick cat in their excitement. By noon they had picked up the last paper napkin, raked over the gravel walks where the salt from the freezers had left white patches, and hung the hammock in which Vickie did her studying back in its place. Mr. Holliday paid the boys a dollar a week for keeping up the yard, and they gave the money to their mother—it didn't come amiss in a family where actual cash was so short. She let them keep half the sum Mrs. Rosen paid for her milk every Saturday, and that was more spending money than most boys had. They often made a few extra quarters by cutting grass for other people, or by distributing handbills. Even the disagreeable Mrs. Jackson next door had remarked over the fence to Mrs. Harris: "I do believe Bert and Del are going to be industrious. They must have got it from you, Grandma."

The day came on very hot, and when the twins got back from the Roadmaster's yard, they both lay down on Grandmother's lounge and went to sleep. After dinner they had a rare opportunity; the Roadmaster himself appeared at the front door and invited them to go up to the next town with him on his railroad velocipede. That was great fun: the velocipede always whizzed along so fast on the bright rails, the gasoline engine puffing; and grasshoppers jumped up out of the sage-brush and hit you in the face like sling-shot bullets. Sometimes the wheels cut in two a lazy snake who was sunning himself on the track, and the twins always hoped it was a rattler and felt they had done a good work.

The boys got back from their trip with Mr. Holliday late in the afternoon. The house was cool and quiet. Their mother had taken Ronald and Hughie down town with her, and Vickie was off somewhere. Grandmother was not in her room, and the kitchen was empty. The boys went out to the back porch to pump a drink. The coal-shed door was open, and inside, on a low stool, sat Mrs. Harris beside her cat. Bert and Del didn't stop to get a drink; they felt ashamed that they had gone off for a gay ride and forgotten Blue Boy. They sat down on a big lump of coal beside Mrs. Harris. They would never have known that this miserable rumpled animal was their proud tom. Presently he went off into a spasm and began to froth at the mouth.

"Oh, Gram'ma, can't you do anything?" cried Albert, struggling with his tears. "Blue Boy was such a good cat,— why has he got to suffer?"

"Everything that's alive has got to suffer," said Mrs. Harris. Albert put out his hand and caught her skirt, looking up at her beseechingly, as if to make her unsay that saying, which he only half understood. She patted his hand. She had forgot she was speaking to a little boy.

"Where's Vickie?" Adelbert asked aggrievedly. "Why don't she do something! He's part her cat."

Mrs. Harris sighed. "Vickie's got her head full of things lately; that makes people kind of heartless."

The boys resolved they would never put anything into their heads, then!

Blue Boy's fit passed, and the three sat watching their pet that no longer knew them. The twins had not seen much suffering; Grandmother had seen a great deal. Back in Tennessee, in her own neighborhood, she was accounted a famous nurse. When any of the poor mountain people were in great distress, they always sent for Miz' Harris. Many a time she had gone into a house where five or six children were all down with scarlet fever or diphtheria, and done what she could. Many a child and many a woman she had laid out and got ready for the grave. In her primitive community the undertaker made the coffin—he did nothing more. She had seen so much misery that she wondered herself why it hurt so to see her tom-cat die. She had taken her leave of him, and she got up from her stool. She didn't want the boys to be too much distressed.

"Now you boys must wash and put on clean shirts. Your mother will be home pretty soon. We'll leave Blue Boy; he'll likely be easier in the morning." She knew the cat would die at sundown.

After supper, when Bert looked into the coal-shed and found the cat dead, all the family were sad. Ronald cried miserably, and Hughie cried because Ronald did. Mrs. Templeton herself went out and looked into the shed, and she was sorry, too. Though she didn't like cats, she had been fond of this one.

"Hillary," she told her husband, "when you go down town tonight, tell the Mexican to come and get that cat early in the morning, before the children are up."

The Mexican had a cart and two mules, and he hauled away tin cans and refuse to a gully out in the sage-brush.

Mrs. Harris gave Victoria an indignant glance when she heard this, and turned back to the kitchen. All evening she was gloomy and silent. She refused to read aloud, and the twins took Ronald and went mournfully out to play under the electric light. Later, when they had said good-night to their parents in the parlor and were on their way upstairs, Mrs. Harris followed them into the kitchen, shut the door behind her, and said indignantly:

"Air you two boys going to let that Mexican take Blue Boy and throw him onto some trash-pile?"

The sleepy boys were frightened at the anger and bitterness in her tone. They stood still and looked up at her, while she went on:

"You git up early in the morning, and I'll put him in a sack, and one of you take a spade and go to that crooked old willer tree that grows just where the sand creek turns off the road, and you dig a little grave for Blue Boy, an' bury him right."

They had seldom seen such resentment in their grandmother. Albert's throat choked up, he rubbed the tears away with his fist.

"Yes'm, Gram'ma, we will, we will," he gulped.

VII

Only Mrs. Harris saw the boys go out next morning. She slipped a bread-and-butter sandwich into the hand of each, but she said nothing, and they said nothing.

The boys did not get home until their parents were ready to leave the table. Mrs. Templeton made no fuss, but told them to sit down and eat their breakfast. When they had finished, she said commandingly:

"Now you march into my room." That was where she heard explanations and administered punishment. When she whipped them, she did it thoroughly.

She followed them and shut the door.

"Now, what were you boys doing this morning?"

"We went off to bury Blue Boy."

"Why didn't you tell me you were going?"

They looked down at their toes, but said nothing. Their mother studied their mournful faces, and her overbearing expression softened.

The next time you get up and go off anywhere, you come and tell me beforehand, do you understand?"

"Yes'm."

She opened the door, motioned them out, and went with them into the parlor. "I'm sorry about your cat, boys," she said. "That's why I don't like to have cats around; they're always getting sick and dying. Now run along and play. Maybe you'd like to have a circus in the back yard this afternoon? And we'll all come."

The twins ran out in a joyful frame of mind. Their grandmother had been mistaken; their mother wasn't indifferent about Blue Boy, she was sorry. Now everything was all right, and they could make a circus ring.

They knew their grandmother got put out about strange things, anyhow. A few months ago it was because their mother hadn't asked one of the visiting preachers who came to the church conference to stay with them. There was no place for the preacher to sleep except on the folding lounge in the parlor, and no place for him to wash—he would have been very uncomfortable, and so would all the household. But Mrs. Harris was terribly upset that there should be a conference in the town, and they not keeping a preacher! She was quite bitter about it.

The twins called in the neighbor boys, and they made a ring in the back yard, around their turning-bar. Their mother came to the show and paid admission, bringing Mrs. Rosen and Grandma Harris. Mrs. Rosen thought if all the children in the neighborhood were to be howling and running in a circle in the Templetons' back yard, she might as well be there, too, for she would have no peace at home.

After the dog races and the Indian fight were over, Mrs. Templeton took Mrs. Rosen into the house to revive her with cake and lemonade. The parlor was cool and dusky. Mrs. Rosen was glad to get into it after sitting on a wooden bench in the sun. Grandmother stayed in the parlor with them, which was unusual. Mrs. Rosen sat waving a palm-leaf fan,—she felt the heat very much, because she wore her stays so tight—while Victoria went to make the lemonade.

"De circuses are not so good, widout Vickie to manage them, Grandma," she said.

"No'm. The boys complain right smart about losing Vickie from their plays. She's at her books all the time now. I don't know what's got into that child."

"If she wants to go to college, she must prepare herself, Grandma. I am agreeably surprised in her. I didn't think she'd stick to it."

Mrs. Templeton came in with a tray of tumblers and the glass pitcher all frosted over. Mrs. Rosen wistfully admired her neighbor's tall figure and good carriage; she was wearing no corsets at all today under her flowered organdie afternoon dress, Mrs. Rosen had noticed, and yet she could carry herself so smooth and straight,—after having had so many children, too! Mrs. Rosen was envious, but she gave credit where credit was due.

When Mrs. Templeton brought in the cake, Mrs. Rosen was still talking to Grandmother about Vickie's studying. Mrs. Templeton shrugged carelessly.

"There's such a thing as overdoing it, Mrs. Rosen," she observed as she poured the lemonade. "Vickie's very apt to run to extremes."

"But, my dear lady, she can hardly be too extreme in dis matter. If she is to take a competitive examination with girls from much better schools than ours, she will have to do better than the others, or fail; no two ways about it. We must encourage her."

Mrs. Templeton bridled a little. "I'm sure I don't interfere with her studying, Mrs. Rosen. I don't see where she got this notion, but I let her alone."

Mrs. Rosen accepted a second piece of chocolate cake. "And what do you think about it, Grandma?"

Mrs. Harris smiled politely. "None of our people, or Mr. Templeton's either, ever went to college. I expect it is all on account of the young gentleman who was here last summer."

Mrs. Rosen laughed and lifted her eyebrows. "Something very personal in Vickie's admiration for Professor Chalmers we think, Grandma? A very sudden interest in de sciences, I should say!"

Mrs. Templeton shrugged. "You're mistaken, Mrs. Rosen. There ain't a particle of romance in Vickie."

"But there are several kinds of romance, Mrs. Templeton. She may not have your kind."

"Yes'm, that's so," said Mrs. Harris in a low, grateful voice. She thought that a hard word Victoria had said of Vickie.

"I didn't see a thing in that Professor Chalmers, myself," Victoria remarked. "He was a gawky kind of fellow, and never had a thing to say in company. Do you think he amounted to much?"

"Oh, widout doubt Doctor Chalmers is a very scholarly man. A great many brilliant scholars are widout de social graces, you know." When Mrs. Rosen, from a much wider experience, corrected her neighbor, she did so somewhat playfully, as if insisting upon something Victoria capriciously chose to ignore.

At this point old Mrs. Harris put her hands on the arms of the chair in preparation to rise. "If you ladies will excuse me, I think I will go and lie down a little before supper." She rose and went heavily out on her felt soles. She never really lay down in the afternoon, but she dozed in her own black rocker. Mrs. Rosen and Victoria sat chatting about Professor Chalmers and his boys.

Last summer the young professor had come to Skyline with four of his students from the University of Michigan, and had stayed three months, digging for fossils out in the sandhills. Vickie had spent a great many mornings at their camp. They lived at the town hotel, and drove out to their camp every day in a light spring-wagon. Vickie used to wait for them at the edge of the town, in front of the Roadmaster's house, and when the spring-wagon came rattling along, the boys would call: "There's our girl!" slow the horses, and give her a hand up. They said she was their mascot, and were very jolly with her. They had a splendid summer,—found a great bed of fossil elephant bones, where a whole herd must once have perished. Later on they came upon the bones of a new kind of elephant, scarcely larger than a pig. They were greatly excited about their finds, and so was Vickie. That was why they liked her. It was they who told her about a memorial scholarship at Ann Arbor, which was open to any girl from Colorado.

VIII

In August Vickie went down to Denver to take her examinations. Mr. Holliday, the Roadmaster, got her a pass, and arranged that she should stay with the family of one of his passenger conductors.

For three days she wrote examination papers along with other contestants, in one of the Denver high schools, proctored by a teacher. Her father had given her five dollars for incidental expenses, and she came home with a box of mineral specimens for the twins, a singing top for Ronald, and a toy burro for Hughie.

Then began days of suspense that stretched into weeks. Vickie went to the post-office every morning, opened her father's combination box, and looked over the letters, long before he got down town,—always hoping there might be a letter from Ann Arbor. The night mail came in at six, and after supper she hurried to the post-office and waited until the shutter at the general-delivery window was drawn back, a signal that the mail had all been "distributed." While the tedious process of distribution was going on, she usually withdrew from the office, full of joking men and cigar smoke, and walked up and down under the big cottonwood trees that overhung the side street. When the crowd of men began to come out, then she knew the mail-bags were empty, and she went in to get whatever letters were in the Templeton box and take them home.

After two weeks went by, she grew down-hearted. Her young professor, she knew, was in England for his vacation. There would be no one at the University of Michigan who was interested in her fate. Perhaps the fortunate contestant had already been notified of her success. She never asked herself, as she walked up and down under the cottonwoods on those summer nights, what she would do if she didn't get the scholarship. There was no alternative. If she didn't get it, then everything was over.

During the weeks when she lived only to go to the post-office, she managed to cut her finger and get ink into the cut. As a result, she had a badly infected hand and had to carry it in a sling. When she walked her nightly beat under the cottonwoods, it was a kind of comfort to feel that finger throb; it was companionship, made her case more complete.

The strange thing was that one morning a letter came, addressed to Miss Victoria Templeton; in a long envelope such as her father called "legal size," with "*University of Michigan*" in the upper left-hand corner. When Vickie took it from the box, such a wave of fright and weakness went through her that she could scarcely get out of the post-office. She hid the letter under her striped blazer and went a weak, uncertain trail down the sidewalk under the big trees. Without seeing anything or knowing what road she took, she got to the Roadmaster's green yard and her hammock, where she always felt not on the earth, yet of it.

Three hours later, when Mrs. Rosen was just tasting one of those clear soups upon which the Templetons thought she wasted so much pains and good meat, Vickie walked in at the kitchen door and said in a low but somewhat unnatural voice:

"Mrs. Rosen, I got the scholarship."

Mrs. Rosen looked up at her sharply, then pushed the soup back to a cooler part of the stove.

"What is dis you say, Vickie? You have heard from de University?"

"Yes'm. I got the letter this morning." She produced it from under her blazer.

Mrs. Rosen had been cutting noodles. She took Vickie's face in two hot, plump hands that were still floury, and looked at her intently. "Is dat true, Vickie? No mistake? I am delighted—and surprised! Yes, surprised. Den you will *be* something, you won't just sit on de front porch." She squeezed the girl's round, good-natured cheeks, as if she could mold them into something definite then and there. "Now you must stay for lunch and tell us all about it. Go in and announce yourself to Mr. Rosen."

Mr. Rosen had come home for lunch and was sitting, a book in his hand, in a corner of the darkened front parlor where a flood of yellow sun streamed in under the dark green blind. He smiled his friendly smile at Vickie and waved her to a seat, making her understand that he wanted to finish his paragraph. The dark engraving of the pointed cypresses and the Roman tomb was on the wall just behind him.

Mrs. Rosen came into the back parlor, which was the dining-room, and began taking things out of the silver-drawer to lay a place for their visitor. She spoke to her husband rapidly in German.

He put down his book, came over, and took Vickie's hand.

"Is it true, Vickie? Did you really win the scholarship?"

"Yes, sir."

He stood looking down at her through his kind, remote smile,—a smile in the eyes, that seemed to come up through layers and layers of something—gentle doubts, kindly reservations.

"Why do you want to go to college, Vickie?" he asked playfully.

"To learn," she said with surprise.

"But why do you want to learn? What do you want to do with it?"

"I don't know. Nothing, I guess."

"Then what do you want it for?"

"I don't know. I just want it."

For some reason Vickie's voice broke there. She had been terribly strung up all morning, lying in the hammock with her eyes tight shut. She had not been home at all, she had wanted to take her letter to the Rosens first. And now one of the gentlest men she knew made her choke by something strange and presageful in his voice.

"Then if you want it without any purpose at all, you will not be disappointed." Mr. Rosen wished to distract her and help her to keep back the tears. "Listen: a great man once said: '*Le but n'est rien; le chemin, c'est tout.*' That means: The end is nothing, the road is all. Let me write it down for you and give you your first French lesson."

He went to the desk with its big silver ink-well, where he and his wife wrote so many letters in several languages, and inscribed the sentence on a sheet of purple paper, in his delicately shaded foreign script, signing under it a name: *J. Michelet*. He brought it back and shook it before Vickie's eyes. "There, keep it to remember me by. Slip it into the envelope with your college credentials,—that is a good place for it." From his delicate smile and the twitch of one eyebrow, Vickie knew he meant her to take it along as an antidote, a corrective for whatever colleges might do to her. But she had always known that Mr. Rosen was wiser than professors.

Mrs. Rosen was frowning, she thought that sentence a bad precept to give any Templeton. Moreover, she always promptly called her husband back to earth when he soared a little; though it was exactly for this transcendental quality of mind that she reverenced him in her heart, and thought him so much finer than any of his successful brothers.

"Luncheon is served," she said in the crisp tone that put people in their places. "And Miss Vickie, you are to eat your tomatoes with an oil dressing, as we do. If you are going off into the world, it is quite time you learn to like things that are everywhere accepted."

Vickie said: "Yes'm," and slipped into the chair Mr. Rosen had placed for her. Today she didn't care what she ate, though ordinarily she thought a French dressing tasted a good deal like castor oil.

IX

Vickie was to discover that nothing comes easily in this world. Next day she got a letter from one of the jolly students of Professor Chalmer's party, who was watching over her case in his chief's absence. He told her the scholarship meant admission to the freshman class without further examinations, and two hundred dollars toward her expenses; she would have to bring along about three hundred more to put her through the year.

She took this letter to her father's office. Seated in his revolving desk-chair, Mr. Templeton read it over several times and looked embarrassed.

"I'm sorry, daughter," he said at last, "but really, just now, I couldn't spare that much. Not this year. I expect next year will be better for us."

"But the scholarship is for this year, Father. It wouldn't count next year. I just have to go in September."

"I really ain't got it, daughter." He spoke, oh so kindly! He had lovely manners with his daughter and his wife. "It's just all I can do to keep the store bills paid up. I'm away behind with Mr. Rosen's bill. Couldn't you study here this winter and get along about as fast? It isn't that I wouldn't like to let you have the money if I had it. And with young children, I can't let my life insurance go."

Vickie didn't say anything more. She took her letter and wandered down Main Street with it, leaving young Mr. Templeton to a very bad half-hour.

At dinner Vickie was silent, but everyone could see she had been crying. Mr. Templeton told *Uncle Remus* stories to keep up the family morale and make the giggly twins laugh. Mrs. Templeton glanced covertly at her daughter from time to time. She was sometimes a little afraid of Vickie, who seemed to her to have a hard streak. If it were a love-affair that the girl was crying about, that would be so much more natural—and more hopeful!

At two o'clock Mrs. Templeton went to the Afternoon Euchre Club, the twins were to have another ride with the

Roadmaster on his velocipede, the little boys took their nap on their mother's bed. The house was empty and quiet. Vickie felt an aversion for the hammock under the cottonwoods where she had been betrayed into such bright hopes. She lay down on her grandmother's lounge in the cluttered play-room and turned her face to the wall.

When Mrs. Harris came in for her rest, and began to wash her face at the tin basin, Vickie got up. She wanted to be alone. Mrs. Harris came over to her while she was still sitting on the edge of the lounge.

"What's the matter, Vickie child?" She put her hand on her granddaughter's shoulder, but Vickie shrank away. Young misery is like that, sometimes.

"Nothing. Except that I can't go to college after all. Papa can't let me have the money."

Mrs. Harris settled herself on the faded cushions of her rocker. "How much is it? Tell me about it, Vickie. Nobody's around."

Vickie told her what the conditions were, briefly and dryly, as if she were talking to an enemy. Everyone was an enemy; all society was against her. She told her grandmother the facts and then went upstairs, refusing to be comforted.

Mrs. Harris saw her disappear through the kitchen door, and then sat looking at the door, her face grave, her eyes stern and sad. A poor factory-made piece of joiner's work seldom has to bear a look of such intense, accusing sorrow; as if that flimsy pretence of "grained" yellow pine were the door shut against all young aspiration.

X

Mrs. Harris had decided to speak to Mr. Templeton, but opportunities for seeing him alone were not frequent. She watched out of the kitchen window, and when she next saw him go into the barn to fork down hay for his horse, she threw an apron over her head and followed him. She waylaid him as he came down from the hayloft.

"Hillary, I want to see you about Vickie. I was wondering if you could lay hand on any of the money you got for the sale of my house back home."

Mr. Templeton was nervous. He began brushing his trousers with a little whisk-broom he kept there, hanging on a nail.

"Why, no'm, Mrs. Harris. I couldn't just conveniently call in any of it right now. You know we had to use part of it to get moved up here from the mines."

"I know. But I thought if there was any left you could get at, we could let Vickie have it. A body'd like to help the child."

"I'd like to, powerful well, Mrs. Harris. I would, indeedy. But I'm afraid I can't manage it right now. The fellers I've loaned to can't pay up this year. Maybe next year—" He was like a little boy trying to escape a scolding, though he had never had a nagging word from Mrs. Harris.

She looked downcast, but said nothing.

"It's all right, Mrs. Harris," he took on his brisk business tone and hung up the brush. "The money's perfectly safe. It's well invested."

Invested; there was a word men always held over women, Mrs. Harris thought, and it always meant they could have none of their own money. She sighed deeply.

"Well, if that's the way it is—" She turned away and went back to the house on her flat heelless slippers, just in time; Victoria was at that moment coming out to the kitchen with Hughie.

"Ma," she said, "can the little boy play out here, while I go down town?"

XI

For the next few days Mrs. Harris was very somber, and she was not well. Several times in the kitchen she was seized with what she called giddy spells, and Mandy had to help her to a chair and give her a little brandy.

"Don't you say nothin', Mandy," she warned the girl. But Mandy knew enough for that.

Mrs. Harris scarcely noticed how her strength was failing, because she had so much on her mind. She was very proud, and she wanted to do something that was hard for her to do. The difficulty was to catch Mrs. Rosen alone.

On the afternoon when Victoria went to her weekly euchre, the old lady beckoned Mandy and told her to run across the alley and fetch Mrs. Rosen for a minute.

Mrs. Rosen was packing her trunk, but she came at once. Grandmother awaited her in her chair in the play-room.

"I take it very kindly of you to come, Mrs. Rosen. I'm afraid it's warm in here. Won't you have a fan?" She extended the palm leaf she was holding.

"Keep it yourself, Grandma. You are not looking very well. Do you feel badly, Grandma Harris?" She took the old lady's hand and looked at her anxiously.

"Oh, no, ma'am! I'm as well as usual. The heat wears on me a little, maybe. Have you seen Vickie lately, Mrs. Rosen?"

"Vickie? No. She hasn't run in for several days. These young people are full of their own affairs, you know."

"I expect she's backward about seeing you, now that she's so discouraged."

"Discouraged? Why, didn't the child get her scholarship after all?"

"Yes'm, she did. But they write her she has to bring more money to help her out; three hundred dollars. Mr. Templeton can't raise it just now. We had so much sickness in that mountain town before we moved up here, he got behind. Pore Vickie's downhearted."

"Oh, that is too bad! I expect you've been fretting over it, and that is why you don't look like yourself. Now what can we do about it?"

Mrs. Harris sighed and shook her head. "Vickie's trying to muster courage to go around to her father's friends and borrow from one and another. But we ain't been here long,—it ain't like we had old friends here. I hate to have the child do it."

Mrs. Rosen looked perplexed. "I'm sure Mr. Rosen would help her. He takes a great interest in Vickie."

"I thought maybe he could see his way to. That's why I sent Mandy to fetch you."

"That was right, Grandma. Now let me think." Mrs. Rosen put up her plump red-brown hand and leaned her chin upon it. "Day after tomorrow I am going on to Chicago for my niece's wedding." She saw her old friend's face fall. "Oh, I shan't be gone long; ten days, perhaps. I will speak to Mr. Rosen tonight, and if Vickie goes to him after I am off his hands, I'm sure he will help her."

Mrs. Harris looked up at her with solemn gratitude. "Vickie ain't the kind of girl would forget anything like that, Mrs. Rosen. Nor I wouldn't forget it."

Mrs. Rosen patted her arm. "Grandma Harris," she exclaimed, "I will just ask Mr. Rosen to do it for you! You know I care more about the old folks than the young. If I take this worry off your mind, I shall go away to the wedding with a light heart. Now dismiss it. I am sure Mr. Rosen can arrange this himself for you, and Vickie won't have to go about to these people here, and our gossipy neighbors will never be the wiser." Mrs. Rosen poured this out in her quick, authoritative tone, converting her *th*'s into *d*'s, as she did when she was excited.

Mrs. Harris's red-brown eyes slowly filled with tears,— Mrs. Rosen had never seen that happen before. But she simply said, with quiet dignity: "Thank you, ma'am. I wouldn't have turned to nobody else."

"That means I am an old friend already, doesn't it, Grandma? And that's what I want to be. I am very jealous where

Grandma Harris is concerned!" She lightly kissed the back of the purple-veined hand she had been holding, and ran home to her packing. Grandma sat looking down at her hand. How easy it was for these foreigners to say what they felt!

XII

Mrs. Harris knew she was failing. She was glad to be able to conceal it from Mrs. Rosen when that kind neighbor dashed in to kiss her good-bye on the morning of her departure for Chicago. Mrs. Templeton was, of course, present, and secrets could not be discussed. Mrs. Rosen, in her stiff little brown traveling-hat, her hands tightly gloved in brown kid, could only wink and nod to Grandmother to tell her all was well. Then she went out and climbed into the "hack" bound for the depot, which had stopped for a moment at the Templetons' gate.

Mrs. Harris was thankful that her excitable friend hadn't noticed anything unusual about her looks, and, above all, that she had made no comment. She got through the day, and that evening, thank goodness, Mr. Templeton took his wife to hear a company of strolling players sing *The Chimes of Normandy* at the Opera House. He loved music, and just now he was very eager to distract and amuse Victoria. Grandma sent the twins out to play and went to bed early.

Next morning, when she joined Mandy in the kitchen, Mandy noticed something wrong.

"You set right down, Miz' Harris, an' let me git you some whisky. Deed, ma'am, you look awful porely. You ought to tell Miss Victoria an' let her send for the doctor."

"No, Mandy, I don't want no doctor. I've seen more sickness than ever he has. Doctors can't do no more than linger you out, an' I've always prayed I wouldn't last to be a burden. You git me some whisky in hot water, and pour it on a piece of toast. I feel real empty."

That afternoon when Mrs. Harris was taking her rest, for once she lay down upon her lounge. Vickie came in, tense and excited, and stopped for a moment.

"It's all right, Grandma. Mr. Rosen is going to lend me the money. I won't have to go to anybody else. He won't ask Father to endorse my note, either. He'll just take my name." Vickie rather shouted this news at Mrs. Harris, as if the old lady were deaf, or slow of understanding. She didn't thank her; she didn't know her grandmother was in any way responsible for Mr. Rosen's offer, though at the close of their interview he had said: "We won't speak of our arrangement to anyone but your father. And I want you to mention it to the old lady Harris. I know she has been worrying about you."

Having brusquely announced her news, Vickie hurried away. There was so much to do about getting ready, she didn't know where to begin. She had no trunk and no clothes. Her winter coat, bought two years ago, was so outgrown that she couldn't get into it. All her shoes were run over at the heel and must go to the cobbler. And she had only two weeks in which to do everything! She dashed off.

Mrs. Harris sighed and closed her eyes happily. She thought with modest pride that with people like the Rosens she had always "got along nicely." It was only with the ill-bred and unclassified, like this Mrs. Jackson next door, that she had disagreeable experiences. Such folks, she told herself, had come out of nothing and knew no better. She was afraid this inquisitive woman might find her ailing and come prying round with unwelcome suggestions.

Mrs. Jackson did, indeed, call that very afternoon, with a miserable contribution of veal-loaf as an excuse (all the Templetons hated veal), but Mandy had been forewarned, and she was resourceful. She met Mrs. Jackson at the kitchen door and blocked the way.

"Sh-h-h, ma'am, Miz' Harris is asleep, havin' her nap. No'm, she ain't porely, she's as usual. But Hughie had the colic last night when Miss Victoria was at the show, an' kep' Miz' Harris awake."

Mrs. Jackson was loath to turn back. She had really come to find out why Mrs. Rosen drove away in the depot hack yesterday morning. Except at church socials, Mrs. Jackson did not meet people in Mrs. Rosen's set.

The next day, when Mrs. Harris got up and sat on the edge of her bed, her head began to swim, and she lay down again. Mandy peeped into the play-room as soon as she came down-stairs, and found the old lady still in bed. She leaned over her and whispered:

"Ain't you feelin' well, Miz' Harris?"

"No, Mandy, I'm right porely," Mrs. Harris admitted.

"You stay right where you air, ma'am. I'll git the breakfast fur the chillun, an' take the other breakfast in fur Miss

Victoria an' Mr. Templeton." She hurried back to the kitch-en, and Mrs. Harris went to sleep.

Immediately after breakfast Vickie dashed off about her own concerns, and the twins went to cut grass while the dew was still on it. When Mandy was taking the other breakfast into the dining-room, Mrs. Templeton came through the play-room.

"What's the matter, Ma? Are you sick?" she asked in an accusing tone.

"No, Victoria, I ain't sick. I had a little giddy spell, and I thought I'd lay still."

"You ought to be more careful what you eat, Ma. If you're going to have another bilious spell, when everything is so upset anyhow, I don't know what I'll do!" Victoria's voice broke. She hurried back into her bedroom, feeling bit-terly that there was no place in that house to cry in, no spot where one could be alone, even with misery; that the house and the people in it were choking her to death.

Mrs. Harris sighed and closed her eyes. Things did seem to be upset, though she didn't know just why. Mandy, how-ever, had her suspicions. While she waited on Mr. and Mrs. Templeton at breakfast, narrowly observing their manner toward each other and Victoria's swollen eyes and desperate expression, her suspicions grew stronger.

Instead of going to his office, Mr. Templeton went to the barn and ran out the buggy. Soon he brought out Cleveland, the black horse, with his harness on. Mandy watched from the back window. After he had hitched the horse to the buggy, he came into the kitchen to wash his hands. While he dried them on the roller towel, he said in his most business-like tone:

"I likely won't be back tonight, Mandy. I have to go out to my farm, and I'll hardly get through my business there in time to come home."

Then Mandy was sure. She had been through these times before, and at such a crisis poor Mr. Templeton was always called away on important business. When he had driven out through the alley and up the street past Mrs. Rosen's, Mandy left her dishes and went in to Mrs. Harris. She bent over and whispered low:

"Miz' Harris, I 'spect Miss Victoria's done found out she's goin' to have another baby! It looks that way. She's gone back to bed."

Mrs. Harris lifted a warning finger. "Sh-h-h!"

"Oh yes'm, I won't say nothin'. I never do."

Mrs. Harris tried to face this possibility, but her mind didn't seem strong enough—she dropped off into another doze.

All that morning Mrs. Templeton lay on her bed alone, the room darkened and a handkerchief soaked in camphor tied round her forehead. The twins had taken Ronald off to watch them cut grass, and Hughie played in the kitchen under Mandy's eye.

Now and then Victoria sat upright on the edge of the bed, beat her hands together softly and looked desperately at the ceiling, then about at those frail, confining walls. If only she could meet the situation with violence, fight it, conquer it! But there was nothing for it but stupid animal patience. She would have to go through all that again, and nobody, not even Hillary, wanted another baby,—poor as they were, and in this overcrowded house. Anyhow, she told herself, she was ashamed to have another baby, when she had a daughter old enough to go to college! She was sick of it all; sick of dragging this chain of life that never let her rest and periodically knotted and overpowered her; made her ill and hideous for months, and then dropped another baby into her arms. She had had babies enough; and there ought to be an end to such apprehensions some time before you were old and ugly.

She wanted to run away, back to Tennessee, and lead a free, gay life, as she had when she was first married. She could do a great deal more with freedom than ever Vickie could. She was still young, and she was still handsome; why must she be for ever shut up in a little cluttered house with children and fresh babies and an old woman and a stupid bound girl and a husband who wasn't very successful? Life hadn't brought her what she expected when she married Hillary Templeton; life hadn't used her right. She had tried to keep up appearances, to dress well with very little to do it on, to keep young for her husband and children. She had tried, she had tried! Mrs. Templeton buried her face in the pillow and smothered the sobs that shook the bed.

Hillary Templeton, on his drive out through the sage-brush, up into the farming country that was irrigated from the North

Platte, did not feel altogether cheerful, though he whistled and sang to himself on the way. He was sorry Victoria would have to go through another time. It was awkward just now, too, when he was so short of money. But he was naturally a cheerful man, modest in his demands upon fortune, and easily diverted from unpleasant thoughts. Before Cleveland had traveled half the eighteen miles to the farm, his master was already looking forward to a visit with his tenants, an old German couple who were fond of him because he never pushed them in a hard year—so far, all the years had been hard—and he sometimes brought them bananas and such delicacies from town.

Mrs. Heyse would open her best preserves for him, he knew, and kill a chicken, and tonight he would have a clean bed in her spare room. She always put a vase of flowers in his room when he stayed overnight with them, and that pleased him very much. He felt like a youth out there, and forgot all the bills he had somehow to meet, and the loans he had made and couldn't collect. The Heyses kept bees and raised turkeys, and had honeysuckle vines running over the front porch. He loved all those things. Mr. Templeton touched Cleveland with the whip, and as they sped along into the grass country, sang softly:

"Old Jesse was a gem'man
Way down in Tennessee."

XIII

Mandy had to manage the house herself that day, and she was not at all sorry. There wasn't a great deal of variety in her life, and she felt very important taking Mrs. Harris's place, giving the children their dinner, and carrying a plate of milk toast to Mrs. Templeton. She was worried about Mrs. Harris, however, and remarked to the children at noon that she thought somebody ought to "set" with their grandma. Vickie wasn't home for dinner. She had her father's office to herself for the day and was making the most of it, writing a long letter to Professor Chalmers. Mr. Rosen had invited her to have dinner with him at the hotel (he boarded there when his wife was away), and that was a great honor.

When Mandy said someone ought to be with the old lady, Bert and Del offered to take turns. Adelbert went off to rake up the grass they had been cutting all morning, and Albert sat down in the play-room. It seemed to him his grandmother looked pretty sick. He watched her while Mandy gave her toast-water with whisky in it, and thought he would like to make the room look a little nicer. While Mrs. Harris lay with her eyes closed, he hung up the caps and coats lying about, and moved away the big rocking-chair that stood by the head of Grandma's bed. There ought to be a table there, he believed, but the small tables in the house all had something on them. Upstairs, in the room where he and Adelbert and Ronald slept, there was a nice clean wooden cracker-box, on which they sat in the morning to put on their shoes and stockings. He brought this down and stood it on end at the head of Grandma's lounge, and put a clean napkin over the top of it.

She opened her eyes and smiled at him. "Could you git me a tin of fresh water, honey?"

He went to the back porch and pumped till the water ran cold. He gave it to her in a tin cup as she had asked, but he didn't think that was the right way. After she dropped back on the pillow, he fetched a glass tumbler from the cupboard, filled it, and set it on the table he had just manufactured. When Grandmother drew a red cotton handkerchief from under her pillow and wiped the moisture from her face, he ran upstairs again and got one of his Sunday-school handkerchiefs, linen ones, that Mrs. Rosen had given him and Del for Christmas. Having put this in Grandmother's hand and taken away the crumpled red one, he could think of nothing else to do—except to darken the room a little. The windows had no blinds, but flimsy cretonne curtains tied back,—not really tied, but caught back over nails driven into the sill. He loosened them and let them hang down over the bright afternoon sunlight. Then he sat down on the low sawed-off chair and gazed about, thinking that now it looked quite like a sick-room.

It was hard for a little boy to keep still. "Would you like me to read *Joe's Luck* to you, Gram'ma?" he said presently.

"You might, Bertie."

He got the "boy's book" she had been reading aloud to them, and began where she had left off. Mrs. Harris liked to hear his voice, and she liked to look at him when she opened her eyes from time to time. She did not follow the story. In her mind she was repeating a passage from the second part of *Pilgrim's Progress*, which she had read aloud to the children so many times; the passage where Christiana and her band come to the arbor on the Hill of Difficulty: "*Then said Mercy, how sweet is rest to them that labor.*"

At about four o'clock Adelbert came home, hot and sweaty from raking. He said he had got in the grass and taken it to their cow, and if Bert was reading, he guessed he'd like to listen. He dragged the wooden rocking-chair up close to Grandma's bed and curled up in it.

Grandmother was perfectly happy. She and the twins were about the same age; they had in common all the realest and truest things. The years between them and her, it seemed to Mrs. Harris, were full of trouble and unimportant. The twins and Ronald and Hughie were important. She opened her eyes.

"Where is Hughie?" she asked.

"I guess he's asleep. Mother took him into her bed."

"And Ronald?"

"He's upstairs with Mandy. There ain't nobody in the kitchen now."

"Then you might git me a fresh drink, Del."

"Yes'm, Gram'ma." He tiptoed out to the pump in his brown canvas sneakers.

When Vickie came home at five o'clock, she went to her mother's room, but the door was locked—a thing she couldn't remember ever happening before. She went into the play-room,—old Mrs. Harris was asleep, with one of the twins on guard, and he held up a warning finger. She went into the kitchen. Mandy was making biscuits, and Ronald was helping her to cut them out.

"What's the matter, Mandy? Where is everybody?"

"You know your papa's away, Miss Vickie; an' your mama's got a headache, an' Miz' Harris has had a bad spell. Maybe I'll just fix supper for you an' the boys in the kitchen, so you won't all have to be runnin' through her room."

"Oh, very well," said Vickie bitterly, and she went upstairs. Wasn't it just like them all to go and get sick, when she had now only two weeks to get ready for school, and no trunk and no clothes or anything? Nobody but Mr. Rosen seemed to take the least interest, "when my whole life hangs by a thread," she told herself fiercely. What were families for, anyway?

After supper Vickie went to her father's office to read; she told Mandy to leave the kitchen door open, and when she got home she would go to bed without disturbing anybody. The twins ran out to play under the electric light with the neighbor boys for a little while, then slipped softly up the back stairs to their room. Mandy came to Mrs. Harris after the house was still.

"Kin I rub your legs fur you, Miz' Harris?"

"Thank you, Mandy. And you might get me a clean nightcap out of the press."

Mandy returned with it.

"Lawsie me! But your legs is cold, ma'am!"

"I expect it's about time, Mandy," murmured the old lady. Mandy knelt on the floor and set to work with a will. It brought the sweat out on her, and at last she sat up and wiped her face with the back of her hand.

"I can't seem to git no heat into 'em, Miz' Harris. I got a hot flat-iron on the stove; I'll wrap it in a piece of old blanket and put it to your feet. Why didn't you have the boys tell me you was cold, pore soul?"

Mrs. Harris did not answer. She thought it was probably a cold that neither Mandy nor the flat-iron could do much with. She hadn't nursed so many people back in Tennessee without coming to know certain signs.

After Mandy was gone, she fell to thinking of her blessings. Every night for years, when she said her prayers, she had prayed that she might never have a long sickness or be a burden. She dreaded the heart-ache and humiliation of being helpless on the hands of people who would be impatient under such a care. And now she felt certain that she was going to die tonight, without troubling anybody.

She was glad Mrs. Rosen was in Chicago. Had she been at home, she would certainly have come in, would have seen that her old neighbor was very sick, and bustled about. Her quick eye would have found out all Grandmother's little secrets: how hard her bed was, that she had no proper place to wash, and kept her comb in her pocket; that her nightgowns were patched and darned. Mrs. Rosen would have been indignant, and that would have made Victoria cross. She didn't have to see Mrs. Rosen again to know that Mrs.

Rosen thought highly of her and admired her—yes, admired her. Those funny little pats and arch pleasantries had meant a great deal to Mrs. Harris.

It was a blessing that Mr. Templeton was away, too. Appearances had to be kept up when there was a man in the house; and he might have taken it into his head to send for the doctor, and stir everybody up. Now everything would be so peaceful. "*The Lord is my shepherd*," she whispered gratefully. "Yes, Lord, I always spoiled Victoria. She was so much the prettiest. But nobody won't ever be the worse for it: Mr. Templeton will always humor her, and the children love her more than most. They'll always be good to her; she has that way with her."

Grandma fell to remembering the old place at home: what a dashing, high-spirited girl Victoria was, and how proud she had always been of her; how she used to hear her laughing and teasing out in the lilac arbor when Hillary Templeton was courting her. Toward morning all these pleasant reflections faded out. Mrs. Harris felt that she and her bed were softly sinking, through the darkness to a deeper darkness.

Old Mrs. Harris did not really die that night, but she believed she did. Mandy found her unconscious in the morning. Then there was a great stir and bustle; Victoria, and even Vickie, were startled out of their intense self-absorption. Mrs. Harris was hastily carried out of the play-room and laid in Victoria's bed, put into one of Victoria's best nightgowns. Mr. Templeton was sent for, and the doctor was sent for. The inquisitive Mrs. Jackson from next door got into the house at last,—installed herself as nurse, and no one had the courage to say her nay. But Grandmother was out of it all, never knew that she was the object of so much attention and excitement. She died a little while after Mr. Templeton got home.

Thus Mrs. Harris slipped out of the Templetons' story; but Victoria and Vickie still had to go on, to follow the long road that leads through things unguessed at and unforesee-able. When they are old, they will come closer and closer to Grandma Harris. They will think a great deal about her, and remember things they never noticed; and their lot will be more or less like hers. They will regret that they heeded her so little; but they, too, will look into the eager, unseeing eyes of young people and feel themselves alone. They will say to themselves: "I was heartless, because I was young and strong and wanted things so much. But now I know."

GUSTAVE FLAUBERT

A SIMPLE HEART

—

I

Madame Aubain's servant Félicité was the envy of the ladies of Pont-l'Évêque for half a century.

She received four pounds a year. For that she was cook and general servant, and did the sewing, washing, and ironing; she could bridle a horse, fatten poultry, and churn butter—and she remained faithful to her mistress, unamiable as the latter was.

Mme. Aubain had married a gay bachelor without money who died at the beginning of 1809, leaving her with two small children and a quantity of debts. She then sold all her property except the farms of Toucques and Geffosses, which brought in two hundred pounds a year at most, and left her house in Saint-Melaine for a less expensive one that had belonged to her family and was situated behind the market.

This house had a slate roof and stood between an alley and a lane that went down to the river. There was an unevenness in the levels of the rooms which made you stumble. A narrow hall divided the kitchen from the "parlor" where Mme. Aubain spent her day, sitting in a wicker easy chair by the window. Against the panels, which were painted white, was a row of eight mahogany chairs. On an old piano under the barometer a heap of wooden and cardboard boxes rose like a pyramid. A stuffed armchair stood on either side of the Louis-Quinze chimneypiece, which was in yellow marble with a clock in the middle of it modelled like a temple of Vesta. The whole room was a little musty, as the floor was lower than the garden.

The first floor began with "Madame's" room: very large, with a pale-flower wallpaper and a portrait of "Monsieur" as a dandy of the period. It led to a smaller room, where there were two children's cots without mattresses. Next came the drawing room, which was always shut up and full of furniture covered with sheets. Then there was a corridor leading to a study. The shelves of a large bookcase were respectably lined with books and papers, and its three wings surrounded a broad writing table in darkwood. The two panels at the end of the room were covered with pen-drawings, watercolor landscapes, and engravings by Audran, all relics of better days and vanished splendor. Félicité's room on the top floor got its light from a dormer-window, which looked over the meadows.

She rose at daybreak to be in time for Mass, and worked

till evening without stopping. Then, when dinner was over, the plates and dishes in order, and the door shut fast, she thrust the log under the ashes and went to sleep in front of the hearth with her rosary in her hand. Félicité was the stubbornest of all bargainers; and as for cleanness, the polish on her saucepans was the despair of other servants. Thrifty in all things, she ate slowly, gathering off the table in her fingers the crumbs of her loaf—a twelve-pound loaf expressly baked for her, which lasted for three weeks.

At all times of year she wore a print handkerchief fastened with a pin behind, a bonnet that covered her hair, grey stockings, a red skirt, and a bibbed apron—such as hospital nurses wear—over her jacket.

Her face was thin and her voice sharp. At twenty-five she looked like forty. From fifty onwards she seemed of no particular age; and with her silence, straight figure, and precise movements she was like a woman made of wood, and going by clockwork.

II

She had had her love-story like another.

Her father, a mason, had been killed by falling off some scaffolding. Then her mother died, her sisters scattered, and a farmer took her in and employed her, while she was still quite little, to herd the cows at pasture. She shivered in rags and would lie flat on the ground to drink water from the ponds; she was beaten for nothing, and finally turned out for the theft of a shilling which she did not steal. She went to another farm, where she became dairy-maid; and as she was liked by her employers her companions were jealous of her.

One evening in August (she was then eighteen) they took her to the assembly at Colleville. She was dazed and stupefied in an instant by the noise of the fiddlers, the lights in the trees, the gay medley of dresses, the lace, the gold crosses, and the throng of people jigging all together. While she kept shyly apart a young man with a well-to-do air, who was leaning on the shaft of a cart and smoking his pipe, came up to ask her to dance. He treated her to cider, coffee, and cake, and bought her a silk handkerchief; and then, imagining she had guessed his meaning, offered to see her home. At the edge of a field of oats he pushed her roughly down. She was frightened and began to cry out; and he went off.

One evening later she was on the Beaumont road. A big hay-wagon was moving slowly along; she wanted to get in front of it, and as she brushed past the wheels she recognized Theodore. He greeted her quite calmly, saying she must excuse it all because it was "the fault of the drink." She could not think of any answer and wanted to run away.

He began at once to talk about the harvest and the worthies of the commune, for his father had left Colleville for the farm at Les Écots, so that now he and she were neighbors. "Ah!" she said. He added that they thought of settling him in life. Well, he was in no hurry; he was waiting for a wife to his fancy. She dropped her head; and then he asked her if she thought of marrying. She answered with a smile that it was mean to make fun of her.

"But I am not, I swear!"—and he passed his left hand round her waist. She walked in the support of his embrace; their steps grew slower. The wind was soft, the stars glittered, the huge wagon-load of hay swayed in front of them, and dust rose from the dragging steps of the four horses. Then, without a word of command, they turned to the right. He clasped her once more in his arms, and she disappeared into the shadow.

The week after Theodore secured some assignations with her.

They met at the end of farmyards, behind a wall, or under a solitary tree. She was not innocent as young ladies are—she had learned knowledge from the animals—but her reason and the instinct of her honor would not let her fall. Her resistance exasperated Theodore's passion; so much so that to satisfy it—or perhaps quite artlessly—he made her an offer of marriage. She was in doubt whether to trust him, but he swore great oaths of fidelity.

Soon he confessed to something troublesome; the year before his parents had bought him a substitute for the army, but any day he might be taken again, and the idea of serving was a terror to him. Félicité took this cowardice of his as a sign of affection, and it redoubled hers. She stole away at night to see him, and when she reached their meeting-place Theodore racked her with his anxieties and urgings.

At last he declared that he would go himself to the prefecture for information, and would tell her the result on the following Sunday, between eleven and midnight.

When the moment came she sped towards her lover. Instead of him she found one of his friends.

He told her that she would not see Theodore any more. To ensure himself against conscription he had married an old woman, Madame Lehoussais, of Toucques, who was very rich.

There was an uncontrollable burst of grief. She threw herself on the ground, screamed, called to the God of mercy, and moaned by herself in the fields till daylight came. Then she came back to the farm and announced that she was going to leave; and at the end of the month she received her wages, tied all her small belongings with a handkerchief, and went to Pont-l'Évêque.

In front of the inn there she made inquiries of a woman in a widow's cap, who, as it happened, was just looking for a cook. The girl did not know much, but her willingness seemed so great and her demands so small that Mme. Aubain ended by saying:

"Very well, then, I will take you."

A quarter of an hour afterwards Félicité was installed in her house.

She lived there at first in a tremble, as it were, at "the style of the house" and the memory of "Monsieur" floating over it all. Paul and Virginie, the first aged seven and the other hardly four, seemed to her beings of a precious substance; she carried them on her back like a horse; it was a sorrow to her that Mme. Aubain would not let her kiss them every minute. And yet she was happy there. Her grief had melted in the pleasantness of things all round.

Every Thursday regular visitors came in for a game of boston, and Félicité got the cards and foot-warmers ready beforehand. They arrived punctually at eight and left before the stroke of eleven.

On Monday mornings the dealer who lodged in the covered passage spread out all his old iron on the ground. Then a hum of voices began to fill the town, mingled with the neighing of horses, bleating of lambs, grunting of pigs, and the sharp rattle of carts along the street. About noon, when the market was at its height, you might see a tall, hook-nosed old countryman with his cap pushed back making his appearance at the door. It was Robelin, the farmer of Geffosses. A little later came Liébard, the farmer from Toucques—short, red, and corpulent—in a gray jacket and gaiters shod with spurs.

Both had poultry or cheese to offer their landlord. Félicité was invariably a match for their cunning, and they went away filled with respect for her.

At vague intervals Mme. Aubain had a visit from the Marquis de Gremanville, one of her uncles, who had ruined himself by debauchery and now lived at Falaise on his last remaining morsel of land. He invariably came at the luncheon hour, with a dreadful poodle whose paws left all the furniture in a mess. In spite of efforts to show his breeding, which he carried to the point of raising his hat every time he mentioned "my late father," habit was too strong for him; he poured himself out glass after glass and fired off improper remarks. Félicité edged him politely out of the house—"You have had enough, Monsieur de Gremanville! Another time!"—and she shut the door on him.

She opened it with pleasure to M. Bourais, who had been a lawyer. His baldness, his white stock, frilled shirt, and roomy brown coat, his way of rounding the arm as he took snuff—his whole person, in fact, created that disturbance of mind which overtakes us at the sight of extraordinary men.

As he looked after the property of "Madame" he remained shut up with her for hours in "Monsieur's" study, though all the time he was afraid of compromising himself. He respected the magistracy immensely, and had some pretensions to Latin.

To combine instruction and amusement he gave the children a geography book made up of a series of prints. They represented scenes in different parts of the world: cannibals with feathers on their heads, a monkey carrying off a young lady, Bedouins in the desert, the harpooning of a whale, and so on. Paul explained these engravings to Félicité; and that, in fact, was the whole of her literary education. The children's education was undertaken by Guyot, a poor creature employed at the town hall, who was famous for his beautiful hand and sharpened his penknife on his boots.

When the weather was bright the household set off early for a day at Geffosses Farm.

Its courtyard is on a slope, with the farmhouse in the middle, and the sea looks like a gray streak in the distance.

Félicité brought slices of cold meat out of her basket, and they breakfasted in a room adjoining the dairy. It was the only surviving fragment of a country house which was now no more. The wallpaper hung in tatters, and quivered in the drafts. Mme. Aubain sat with bowed head, overcome by her memories; the children became afraid to speak. "Why don't you play, then?" she would say, and off they went.

Paul climbed into the barn, caught birds, played at ducks and drakes over the pond, or hammered with his stick on the big casks which boomed like drums. Virginie fed the rabbits or dashed off to pick cornflowers, her quick legs showing their embroidered little drawers.

One autumn evening they went home by the fields. The moon was in its first quarter, lighting part of the sky; and mist floated like a scarf over the windings of the Toucques. Cattle, lying out in the middle of the grass, looked quietly at the four people as they passed. In the third meadow some of them got up and made a half-circle in front of the walkers. "There's nothing to be afraid of," said Félicité, as she stroked the nearest on the back with a kind of crooning song; he wheeled round and the others did the same. But when they crossed the next pasture there was a formidable bellow. It was a bull, hidden by the mist. Mme. Aubain was about to run. "No! no! don't go so fast!" They mended their pace, however, and heard a loud breathing behind them which came nearer. His hoofs thudded on the meadow grass like hammers; why, he was galloping now! Félicité turned round, and tore up clods of earth with both hands and threw them in his eyes. He lowered his muzzle, waved his horns, and quivered with fury, bellowing terribly. Mme. Aubain, now at the end of the pasture with her two little ones, was looking wildly for a place to get over the high bank. Félicité was retreating, still with her face to the bull, keeping up a shower of clods which blinded him, and crying all the time, "Be quick! be quick!"

Mme. Aubain went down into the ditch, pushed Virginie first and then Paul, fell several times as she tried to climb the bank, and managed it at last by dint of courage.

The bull had driven Félicité to bay against a rail-fence; his slaver was streaming into her face; another second, and he would have gored her. She had just time to slip between two of the rails, and the big animal stopped short in amazement.

This adventure was talked of at Pont-l'Évêque for many a year. Félicité did not pride herself on it in the least, not having the barest suspicion that she had done anything heroic.

Virginie was the sole object of her thoughts, for the child developed a nervous complaint as a result of her fright, M. Poupart, the doctor, advised sea-bathing at Trouville. It was not a frequented place then. Mme. Aubain collected information, consulted Bourais, and made preparations as though for a long journey.

Her luggage started a day in advance, in Liébard's cart. The next day he brought round two horses, one of which had a lady's saddle with a velvet back to it, while a cloak was rolled up to make a kind of seat on the crupper of the other. Mme. Aubain rode on that, behind the farmer. Félicité took charge of Virginie, and Paul mounted M. Lechaptois' donkey, lent on condition that great care was taken of it.

The road was so bad that its five mile took two hours. The horses sank in the mud up to their pasterns, and their haunches jerked abruptly in the effort to get out; or else they stumbled in the ruts, and at other moments had to jump. In some places Liébard's mare came suddenly to a halt. He waited patiently until she went on again, talking about the people who had properties along the road, and adding moral reflections to their history. So it was that as they were in the middle of Toucques, and passed under some windows bowered with nasturtiums, he shrugged his shoulders and said: "There's a Mme. Lehoussais lives there; instead of taking a young man she . . ." Félicité did not hear the rest; the horses were trotting and the donkey galloping. They all turned down a bypath; a gate swung open and two boys appeared; and the party dismounted in front of a manure heap at the very threshold of the farmhouse door.

When Mme. Liébard saw her mistress she gave lavish signs of joy. She served her a luncheon with a sirloin of beef, tripe, black-pudding, a fricassee of chicken, sparkling cider, a fruit tart, and brandied plums; seasoning it all with compliments to Madame, who seemed in better health; Mademoiselle, who was "splendid" now; and Monsieur Paul, who had "filled out" wonderfully. Nor did she forget their deceased grandparents, whom the Liébards had known, as

they had been in the service of the family for several genera-
tions. The farm, like them, had the stamp of antiquity. The
beams on the ceiling were worm-eaten, the walls blackened
with smoke, and the window-panes gray with dust. There
was an oak dresser laden with every sort of useful article—
jugs, plates, pewter bowls, wolf-traps, and sheep-shears; and
a huge syringe made the children laugh. There was not a
tree in the three courtyards without mushrooms growing at
the bottom of it or a tuft of mistletoe on its boughs. Several
of them had been thrown down by the wind. They had
taken root again at the middle; and all were bending under
their wealth of apples. The thatched roofs, like brown velvet
and of varying thickness, withstood the heaviest squalls. The
cart-shed, however, was falling into ruin. Mme. Aubain said
she would see about it, and ordered the animals to be saddled
again.

It was another half-hour before they reached Trouville.
The little caravan dismounted to pass Écores—it was an
overhanging cliff with boats below it—and three minutes
later they were at the end of the quay and entered the courtyard of the Golden Lamb, kept by good Mme. David.

From the first days of their stay Virginie began to feel
less weak, thanks to the change of air and the effect of the
sea-baths. These, for want of a bathing-dress, she took in
her chemise; and her nurse dressed her afterwards in a coast-
guard's cabin which was used by the bathers.

In the afternoons they took the donkey and went off
beyond the Black Rocks, in the directions of Hennequeville.

The path climbed at first through ground with dells in it like the green sward of a park, and then reached a plateau where grass fields and arable lay side by side. Hollies rose stiffly out of the briary tangle at the edge of the road; and here and there a great withered tree made zigzags in the blue air with its branches.

They nearly always rested in a meadow, with Deauville on their left, Havre on their right, and the open sea in front. It glittered in the sunshine, smooth as a mirror and so quiet that its murmur was scarcely to be heard; sparrows chirped in hiding and the immense sky arched over it all. Mme. Aubain sat doing her needlework; Virginie plaited rushes by her side; Félicité pulled up lavender, and Paul was bored and anxious to start home.

Other days they crossed the Toucques in a boat and looked for shells. When the tide went out sea-urchins, star-fish, and jelly-fish were left exposed; and the children ran in pursuit of the foam-flakes which scudded in the wind. The sleepy waves broke on the sand and unrolled all along the beach; it stretched away out of sight, bounded on the land-side by the dunes which parted it from the Marsh, a wide meadow shaped like an arena. As they came home that way, Trouville, on the hill-slope in the background, grew bigger at every step, and its miscellaneous throng of houses seemed to break into a gay disorder.

On days when it was too hot they did not leave their room. From the dazzling brilliance outside light fell in streaks between the laths of the blinds. There were no sounds in the village; and on the pavement below not a soul. This silence round them deepened the quietness of things. In the distance, where men were caulking, there was a tap of hammers as they plugged the hulls, and a sluggish breeze wafted up the smell of tar.

The chief amusement was the return of the fishing-boats. They began to tack as soon as they had passed the buoys. The sails came down on two of the three masts; and they drew on with the foresail swelling like a balloon, glided through the splash of the waves, and when they had reached the middle of the harbor suddenly dropped anchor. Then the boats drew up against the quay. The sailors threw quivering fish over the side; a row of carts was waiting, and women in cotton bonnets darted out to take the baskets and give their men a kiss.

One of them came up to Félicité one day, and she entered the lodgings a little later in a state of delight. She had found a sister again—and then Nastasie Barette, "wife of Leroux," appeared, holding an infant at her breast and another child with her right hand, while on her left was a little cabin boy with his hands on his hips and a cap over his ear.

After a quarter of an hour Mme. Aubain sent them off; but they were always to be found hanging about the kitchen, or encountered in the course of a walk. The husband never appeared.

Félicité was seized with affection for them. She bought them a blanket, some shirts, and a stove; it was clear that they were making a good thing out of her. Mme. Aubain was annoyed by this weakness of hers, and she did not like the liberties taken by the nephew, who said "thee" and "thou" to Paul. So as Virginie was coughing and the fine weather gone, she returned to Pont l'Évêque.

There M. Bourais enlightened her on the choice of a boys' school. The one at Caen was reputed to be the best, and Paul was sent to it. He said his good-byes bravely, content enough at going to live in a house where he would have companions.

Mme. Aubain resigned herself to her son's absence as a thing that had to be. Virginie thought about it less and less. Félicité missed the noise he made. But she found an occupation to distract her; from Christmas onward she took the little girl to catechism every day.

III

After making a genuflexion at the door she walked up between the double row of chairs under the lofty nave, opened Mme. Aubain's pew, sat down, and began to look about her. The choir stalls were filled with the boys on the right and the girls on the left, and the curé stood by the lectern. On a painted window in the apse the Holy Ghost looked down upon the Virgin. Another window showed her on her knees before the child Jesus, and a group carved in wood behind the altar-shrine represented St. Michael overthrowing the dragon.

The priest began with a sketch of sacred history. The Garden, the Flood, the Tower of Babel, cities in flames, dying nations, and overturned idols passed like a dream before her eyes; and the dizzying vision left her with reverence for the Most High and fear of his wrath. Then she wept at the story of the Passion. Why had they crucified Him, when He loved the children, fed the multitudes, healed the blind, and had willed, in His meekness, to be born among the poor, on the dung-heap of a stable? The sowings, harvests, wine-presses, all the familiar things the Gospel speaks of, were a part of her life. They had been made holy by God's passing; and she loved the lambs more tenderly for her love of the Lamb, and the doves because of the Holy Ghost.

She found it hard to imagine Him in person, for He was not merely a bird, but a flame as well, and a breath at other times. It may be His light, she thought, which flits at night about the edge of the marshes, His breathing which drives on the clouds, His voice which gives harmony to the bells; and she would sit rapt in adoration, enjoying the cool walls and the quiet of the church.

Of doctrines she understood nothing—did not even try to understand. The curé discoursed, the children repeated their lesson, and finally she went to sleep, waking up with a start when their wooden shoes clattered on the flagstones as they went away.

It was thus that Félicité, whose religious education had been neglected in her youth, learned the catechism by dint of hearing it; and from that time she copied all Virginie's observances, fasting as she did and confessing with her. On Corpus Christi Day they made a festal altar together.

The first communion loomed distractingly ahead. She fussed over the shoes, the rosary, the book and gloves; and how she trembled as she helped Virginie's mother to dress her!

All through the mass she was racked with anxiety. She could not see one side of the choir because of M. Bourais; but straight in front of her was the flock of maidens, with white crowns above their hanging veils, making the impression of a field of snow; and she knew her dear child at a distance by her dainty neck and thoughtful air. The bell tinkled. The heads bowed, and there was silence. As the organ pealed, singers and congregation took up the "Agnus Dei"; then the procession of the boys began, and after them the girls rose. Step by step, with their hands joined in prayer, they went towards the lighted altar, knelt on the first step, received the sacrament in turn, and came back in the same order to their places. When Virginie's turn came Félicité leaned forward to see her; and with the imaginativeness of deep and tender feeling it seemed to her that she actually was the child; Virginie's face became hers, she was dressed in her clothes, it was her heart beating in her breast. As the moment came to open her mouth she closed her eyes and nearly fainted.

She appeared early in the sacristy next morning for Monsieur the curé to give her the communion. She took it with devotion, but it did not give her the same exquisite delight.

Mme. Aubain wanted to make her daughter into an accomplished person; and as Guyot could not teach her music or English she decided to place her in the Ursuline Convent at Honfleur as a boarder. The child made no objection. Félicité sighed and thought that Madame lacked feeling. Then she reflected that her mistress might be right; matters of this kind were beyond her.

So one day an old spring-van drew up at the door, and out of it stepped a nun to fetch the young lady. Félicité hoisted the luggage on to the top, admonished the driver, and put six pots of preserves, a dozen pears, and a bunch of violets under the seat.

At the last moment Virginie broke into a fit of sobbing; she threw her arms round her mother, who kissed her on the forehead, saying over and over "Come, be brave! be brave!" The step was raised, and the carriage drove off.

Then Mme. Aubain's strength gave way; and in the evening all her friends—the Lormeau family, Mme. Lechaptois, the Rochefeuille ladies, M. de Houppeville, and Bourais—came in to console her.

To be without her daughter was very painful for her at first. But she heard from Virginie three times a week, wrote to her on the other days, walked in the garden, and so filled up the empty hours.

From sheer habit Félicité went into Virginie's room in the mornings and gazed at the walls. It was boredom to her not to have to comb the child's hair now, lace up her boots, tuck her into bed—and not to see her charming face perpetually and hold her hand when they went out together. In this idle condition she tried making lace. But her fingers were too heavy and broke the threads; she could not attend to anything, she had lost her sleep, and was, in her own words, "destroyed."

To "divert herself" she asked leave to have visits from her nephew Victor.

He arrived on Sundays after mass, rosy-cheeked, bare-chested, with the scent of the country he had walked through still about him. She laid her table promptly and they had lunch, sitting opposite each other. She ate as little as possible herself to save expense, but stuffed him with food so generously that at last he went to sleep. At the first stroke of vespers she woke him up, brushed his trousers, fastened his tie, and went to church, leaning on his arm with maternal pride.

Victor was always instructed by his parents to get something out of her—a packet of moist sugar, it might be, a cake of soap, spirits, or even money at times. He brought his things for her to mend and she took over the task, only too glad to have a reason for making him come back.

In August his father took him off on a coasting voyage. It was holiday time, and she was consoled by the arrival of the children. Paul, however, was getting selfish, and Virginie was too old to be called "thou" any longer; this put a constraint and barrier between them.

Victor went to Morlaix, Dunkirk, and Brighton, in succession and made Félicité a present on his return from each voyage. It was a box made of shells the first time, a coffee cup the next, and on the third occasion a large gingerbread man. Victor was growing handsome. He was well made, had a hint of a moustache, good honest eyes, and a small leather hat pushed backwards like a pilot's. He entertained her by telling stories embroidered with nautical terms.

On a Monday, July 14, 1819 (she never forgot the date), he told her that he had signed on for the big voyage and next night but one he would take the Honfleur boat and join his schooner, which was to weight anchor from Havre before long. Perhaps he would be gone two years.

The prospect of this long absence threw Félicité into deep distress; one more good-bye she must have, and on the Wednesday evening, when Madame's dinner was finished, she put on her clogs and made short work of the twelve miles between Pont-l'Évêque and Honfleur.

When she arrived in front of the Calvary she took the turn to the right instead of the left, got lost in the timber-yards, and retraced her steps; some people to whom she spoke advised her to be quick. She went all round the harbor basin, full of ships, and knocked against hawsers; then the ground fell away, lights flashed across each other, and she thought her wits had left her, for she saw horses up in the sky.

Others were neighing by the quay-side, frightened at the sea. They were lifted by a tackle and deposited in a boat, where passengers jostled each other among cider casks, cheese baskets, and sacks of grain; fowls could be heard clucking, the captain swore; and a cabin-boy stood leaning over the bows, indifferent to it all. Félicité, who had not recognized him, called "Victor!" and he raised his head; all at once, as she was darting forwards, the gangway was drawn back.

The Honfleur packet, women singing as they hauled it, passed out of harbor. Its framework creaked and the heavy waves whipped its bows. The canvas had swung round, no one could be seen on board now; and on the moon-silvered sea the boat made a black speck which paled gradually, dipped, and vanished.

As Félicité passed by the Calvary she had a wish to commend to God what she cherished most, and she stood there praying a long time with her face bathed in tears and her eyes towards the clouds. The town was asleep, coastguards were walking to and fro; and water poured without cessation through the holes in the sluice, with the noise of a torrent. The clocks struck two.

The convent parlor would not be open before day. If Félicité were late Madame would most certainly be annoyed; and in spite of her desire to kiss the other child she turned home. The maids at the inn were waking up as she came in to Pont-l'Évêque.

So the poor slip of a boy was going to toss for months and months at sea! She had not been frightened by his previous voyages. From England or Brittany you came back safe enough; but America, the colonies, the islands—these were lost in a dim region at the other end of the world.

Félicité's thoughts from that moment ran entirely on her nephew. On sunny days she was harassed by the idea of thirst; when there was a storm she was afraid of the lightning on his account. As she listened to the wind growling in the chimney or carrying off the slates she pictured him lashed by that same tempest, at the top of a shattered mast, with his body thrown backwards under a sheet of foam; or else (with a reminiscence of the illustrated geography) he was being eaten by savages, captured in a wood by monkeys, or dying on a desert shore. And never did she mention her anxieties.

Mme. Aubain had anxieties of her own, about her daughter. The good sisters found her an affectionate but delicate child. The slightest emotion unnerved her. She had to give up the piano.

Her mother stipulated for regular letters from the convent. She lost patience one morning when the postman did not come, and walked to and fro in the parlor from her armchair to the window. It was really amazing; not a word for four days!

To console Mme. Aubain by her own example Félicité remarked:

"As for me, Madame, it's six months since I heard . . ."

"From whom, pray?"

"Why . . . from my nephew," the servant answered gently.

"Oh! your nephew!" And Mme. Aubain resumed her walk with a shrug of the shoulders, as much to say: "I was not thinking of him! And what is more, it's absurd! A scamp of a cabin-boy—what does he matter? . . . whereas my daughter . . . why, just think!"

Félicité, though she had been brought up on harshness,

felt indignant with Madame—and then forgot. It seemed the simplest thing in the world to her to lose one's head over the little girl. For her the two children were equally important; a bond in her heart made them one, and their destinies must be the same.

She heard from the chemist that Victor's ship had arrived at Havana. He had read this piece of news in a gazette.

Cigars—they made her imagine Havana as a place where no one does anything but smoke, and there was Victor moving among the Negroes in a cloud of tobacco. Could you, she wondered, "in case you needed," return by land? What was the distance from Pont-l'Évêque? She questioned M. Bourais to find out.

He reached for his atlas and began explaining the longitudes; Félicité's consternation provoked a fine pedantic smile. Finally he marked with his pencil a black, imperceptible point in the indentations of an oval spot, and said as he did so, "Here it is." She bent over the map; the maze of colored lines wearied her eyes without conveying anything; and on an invitation from Bourais to tell him her difficulty she begged him to show her the house where Victor was living. Bourais threw up his arms, sneezed, and laughed immensely: a simplicity like hers was a positive joy. And Félicité did not understand the reason; how could she when she expected, very likely, to see the actual image of her nephew—so stunted was her mind!

A fortnight afterwards Liébard came into the kitchen at market-time as usual and handed her a letter from her brother-in-law. As neither of them could read she took it to her mistress.

Mme. Aubain, who was counting the stitches in her knitting, put the work down by her side, broke the seal of her letter, started, and said in a low voice, with a look of meaning:

"It is bad news . . . that they have to tell you. Your nephew . . ."

He was dead. The letter said no more.

Félicité fell on to a chair, leaning her head against the wainscot; and she closed her eyelids, which suddenly flushed pink. Then with bent forehead, hands hanging, and fixed eyes, she said at intervals:

"Poor little lad! poor little lad!"

Liébard watched her and heaved sighs. Mme. Aubain trembled a little.

She suggested that Félicité should go to see her sister at Trouville. Félicité answered by a gesture that she had no need.

There was a silence. The worthy Liébard thought it was time for them to withdraw.

Then Félicité said:

"They don't care, not they!"

Her head dropped again; and she took up mechanically, from time to time, the long needles on her work-table.

Women passed in the yard with a barrow of dripping linen.

As she saw them through the window-panes she remembered her washing; she had put it to soak the day before, to-day she must wring it out; and she left the room.

Her plank and tub were at the edge of the Toucques. She threw a pile of linen on the bank, rolled up her sleeves, and taking her wooden beater dealt lusty blows whose sound carried to the neighboring gardens. The meadows were empty, the river stirred in the wind; and down below long grasses wavered, like the hair of corpses floating in the water. She kept her grief down and was very brave until the evening; but once in her room she surrendered to it utterly, lying stretched on the mattress with her face in the pillow and her hands clenched against her temples.

Much later she heard, from the captain himself, the circumstances of Victor's end. They had bled him too much at the hospital for yellow fever. Four doctors held him at once. He had died instantly, and the chief had said:

"Bah! there goes another!"

His parents had always been brutal to him. She preferred not to see them again; and they made no advances, either because they forgot her or from the callousness of the wretchedly poor.

Virginie began to grow weaker.

Tightness in her chest, coughing, continual fever, and veinings on her cheek-bones betrayed some deep-seated complaint. M. Poupart had advised a stay in Provence. Mme. Aubain determined on it, and would have brought her daughter home at once but for the climate of Pont-l'Évêque.

She made an arrangement with a job-master, and he drove her to the convent every Tuesday. There is a terrace in the garden, with a view over the Seine. Virginie took walks there over the fallen vine-leaves, on her mother's arm. A shaft of sunlight through the clouds made her blink sometimes, as she gazed at the sails in the distance and the whole horizon from the castle of Tancarville to the lighthouses at Havre. Afterwards they rested in the arbor. Her mother had secured a little cask of excellent Malaga; and Virginie, laughing at the idea of getting tipsy, drank a thimble-full of it, no more.

Her strength came back visibly. The autumn glided gently away. Félicité reassured Mme. Aubain. But one evening, when she had been out on a commission in the neighborhood, she found M. Poupart's gig at the door. He was in the hall, and Mme. Aubain was tying her bonnet.

"Give me my foot-warmer, purse, gloves! Quicker, come!"

Virginie had inflammation of the lungs; perhaps it was hopeless.

"Not yet!" said the doctor, and they both got into the carriage under whirling flakes of snow. Night was coming on and it was very cold.

Félicité rushed into the church to light a taper. Then she ran after the gig, came up with it in an hour, and jumped lightly in behind. As she hung on by the fringes a thought came into her mind: "The courtyard has not been shut up; supposing burglars got in!" And she jumped down.

At dawn next day she presented herself at the doctor's. He had come in and started for the country again. Then she waited in the inn, thinking that a letter would come by some hand or other. Finally, when it was twilight, she took the Lisieux coach.

The convent was at the end of a steep lane. When she was about half-way up it she heard strange sounds—a death-bell tolling. "It is for someone else," thought Félicité, and she pulled the knocker violently.

After some minutes there was a sound of trailing slippers, the door opened ajar, and a nun appeared.

The good sister, with an air of compunction, said that "she had just passed away." On the instant the bell of St. Leonard's tolled twice as fast.

Félicité went up to the second floor.

From the doorway she saw Virginie stretched on her back, with her hands joined, her mouth open, and head thrown back under a black crucifix that leaned towards her, between curtains that hung stiffly, less pale than was her face. Mme. Aubain, at the foot of the bed which she clasped with her arms, was choking with sobs of agony. The mother superior stood on the right. Three candlesticks on the chest of drawers made spots of red, and the mist came whitely through the windows. Nuns came and took Mme. Aubain away.

For two nights Félicité never left the dead child. She repeated the same prayers, sprinkled holy water over the sheets, came and sat down again, and watched her. At the end of the first vigil she noticed that the face had grown yellow, the lips turned blue, the nose was sharper, and the eyes sunk in. She kissed them several times, and would not have been immensely surprised if Virginie had opened them again; to minds like hers the supernatural is quite simple. She made the girl's toilette, wrapped her in her shroud, lifted her down into her bier, put a garland on her head, and spread out her hair. It was fair, and extraordinarily long for her age. Félicité cut off a big lock and slipped half of it into her bosom, determined that she should never part with it.

The body was brought back to Pont-l'Évêque, as Mme. Aubain intended; she followed the hearse in a closed carriage.

It took another three-quarters of an hour after the mass to reach the cemetery. Paul walked in front, sobbing. M. Bourais was behind, and then came the chief residents, the women shrouded in black mantles, and Félicité. She thought of her nephew; and because she had not been able to pay these honors to him her grief was doubled, as though the one were being buried with the other.

Mme. Aubain's despair was boundless. It was against God that she first rebelled, thinking it unjust of Him to have taken her daughter from her—she had never done evil and her conscience was so clear! Ah, no!—she ought to have taken Virginie off to the south. Other doctors would have saved her. She accused herself now, wanted to join her child, and broke into cries of distress in the middle of her dreams. One dream haunted her above all. Her husband, dressed as a sailor, was returning from a long voyage, and shedding tears he told her that he had been ordered to take Virginie away. Then they consulted how to hide her somewhere.

She came in once from the garden quite upset. A moment ago—and she pointed out the place—the father and daughter had appeared to her, standing side by side, and they did nothing, but they looked at her.

For several months after this she stayed inertly in her room. Félicité lectured her gently; she must live for her son's sake, and for the other, in remembrance of "her."

"Her?" answered Mme. Aubain, as though she were just waking up. "Ah, yes! . . . yes! . . . You do not forget her!" This was an allusion to the cemetery, where she was strictly forbidden to go.

Félicité went there every day.

Precisely at four she skirted the houses, climbed the hill, opened the gate, and came to Virginie's grave. It was a little column of pink marble with a stone underneath and a garden plot enclosed by chains. The beds were hidden under a coverlet of flowers. She watered their leaves, freshened the gravel, and knelt down to break up the earth better. When Mme. Aubain was able to come there she felt a relief and a sort of consolation.

Then years slipped away, one like another, and their only episodes were the great festivals as they recurred— Easter, the Assumption, All Saints' Day. Household occurrences marked dates that were referred to afterwards. In 1825, for instance, two glaziers whitewashed the hall; in

1827 a piece of the roof fell into the courtyard and nearly killed a man. In the summer of 1828 it was Madame's turn to offer the consecrated bread; Bourais, about this time, mysteriously absented himself; and one by one the old acquaintances passed away: Guyot, Liébard, Mme. Lechaptois, Robelin, and Uncle Gremanville, who had been paralyzed for a long time.

One night the driver of the mail-coach announced the Revolution of July in Pont-l'Évêque. A new sub-prefect was appointed a few days later—Baron de Larsonnière, who had been consul in America, and brought with him, besides his wife, a sister-in-law and three young ladies, already growing up. They were to be seen about on their lawn, in loose blouses, and they had a Negro and a parrot. They paid a call on Mme. Aubain which she did not fail to return. The moment they were seen in the distance Félicité ran to let her mistress know. But only one thing could really move her feelings—the letters from her son.

He was swallowed up in a tavern life and could follow no career. She paid his debts, he made new ones; and the sighs that Mme. Aubain uttered as she sat knitting by the window reached Félicité at her spinning-wheel in the kitchen.

They took walks together along the espaliered wall, always talking of Virginie and wondering if such and such a thing would have pleased her and what, on some occasion, she would have been likely to say.

All her small belongings filled a cupboard in the two-bedded room. Mme. Aubain inspected them as seldom as

she could. One summer day she made up her mind to it—
and some moths flew out of the wardrobe.

Viginie's dresses were in a row underneath a shelf, on
which there were three dolls, some hoops, a set of toy pots
and pans, and the basin that she used. They took out her pet-
ticoats as well, and the stockings and handkerchiefs, and laid
them out on the two beds before folding them up again. The
sunshine lit up these poor things, bringing out their stains
and the creases made by the body's movements. The air was
warm and blue, a blackbird warbled, life seemed bathed in
a deep sweetness. They found a little plush hat with thick,
chestnut-colored pile; but it was eaten all over by moth.
Félicité begged it for her own. Their eyes met fixedly and
filled with tears; at last the mistress opened her arms, the servant threw herself into them, and they embraced each other,
satisfying their grief in a kiss that made them equal.

It was the first time in their lives, Mme. Aubain's nature
not being expansive. Félicité was as grateful as though she
had received a favor, and cherished her mistress from that
moment with the devotion of an animal and a religious wor-
ship.

The kindness of her heart unfolded.

When she heard the drums of a marching regiment
in the street she posted herself at the door with a pitcher
of cider and asked the soldiers to drink. She nursed chol-
era patients and protected the Polish refugees; one of these
even declared that he wished to marry her. They quarreled,
however; for when she came back from the Angelus one

morning she found that he had got into her kitchen and made himself a vinegar salad which he was quietly eating.

After the Poles came father Colmiche, an old man who was supposed to have committed atrocities in '93. He lived by the side of the river in the ruins of a pigsty. The little boys watched him through the cracks in the wall, and threw pebbles at him which fell on the pallet where he lay constantly shaken by a catarrh; his hair was very long, his eyes inflamed, and there was a tumor on his arm bigger than his head. She got him some linen and tried to clean up his miserable hole; her dream was to establish him in the bakehouse, without letting him annoy Madame. When the tumor burst she dressed it every day; sometimes she brought him cake, and would put him in the sunshine on a truss of straw. The poor old man, slobbering and trembling, thanked her in his worn-out voice, was terrified that he might lose her, and stretched out his hands when he saw her go away. He died; and she had a mass said for the repose of his soul.

That very day a great happiness befell her; just at dinnertime appeared Mme. de Larsonnière's Negro, carrying the parrot in its cage, with perch, chain, and padlock. A note from the baroness informed Mme. Aubain that her husband had been raised to a prefecture and they were starting that evening; she begged her to accept the bird as a memento and mark of her regard.

For a long time he had absorbed Félicité's imagination, because he came from America; and that name reminded her of Victor, so much so that she made inquiries of the Negro.

She had once gone so far as to say "How Madame would enjoy having him!"

The Negro repeated the remark to his mistress; and as she could not take the bird away with her she chose this way of getting rid of him.

IV

His name was Loulou. His body was green and the tips of his wings rose-pink; his forehead was blue and his throat golden.

But he had the tiresome habits of biting his perch, tearing out his feathers, sprinkling his dirt about, and spattering the water of his tub. He annoyed Mme. Aubain, and she gave him to Félicité for good.

She endeavored to train him; soon he could repeat "Nice boy! Your servant, sir! Good morning, Marie!" He was placed by the side of the door, and astonished several people by not answering to the name Jacquot, for all parrots are called Jacquot. People compared him to a turkey and a log of wood, and stabbed Félicité to the heart each time. Strange obstinacy on Loulou's part!—directly you looked at him he refused to speak.

None the less he was eager for society; for on Sundays, while the Rochefeuille ladies, M. de Houppeville, and new familiars—Onfroy the apothecary, Monsieur Varin, and Captain Mathieu—were playing their game of cards, he beat the windows with his wings and threw himself about so frantically that they could not hear each other speak.

Bourais' face, undoubtedly, struck him as extremely droll. Directly he saw it he began to laugh—and laugh with all his might. His peals rang through the courtyard and were repeated by the echo; the neighbors came to their windows and laughed too; while M. Bourais, gliding along under the wall to escape the parrot's eye, and hiding his profile with his hat, got to the river and then entered by the garden gate. There was a lack of tenderness in the looks which he darted at the bird.

Loulou had been slapped by the butcher-boy for making so free as to plunge his head into his basket; and since then he was always trying to nip him through his shirt. Fabu threatened to wring his neck, although he was not cruel, for all his tattooed arms and large whiskers. Far from it; he really rather liked the parrot, and in a jovial humor even wanted to teach him to swear. Félicité, who was alarmed by such proceedings, put the bird in the kitchen. His little chain was taken off and he roamed about the house.

His way of going downstairs was to lean on each step with the curve of his beak, raise the right foot, and then the left; and Félicité was afraid that these gymnastics brought on fits of giddiness. He fell ill and could not talk or eat any longer. There was a growth under his tongue, such as fowls have sometimes. She cured him by tearing the pellicle off with her finger-nails. Mr. Paul was thoughtless enough one day to blow some cigar smoke into his nostrils, and another time when Mme. Lormeau was teasing him with the end of her umbrella he snapped at the ferrule. Finally he got lost.

Félicité had put him on the grass to refresh him, and gone away for a minute, and when she came back—no sign of the parrot! She began by looking for him in the shrubs, by the waterside, and over the roofs, without listening to her mistress's cries of "Take care, do! You are out of your wits!" Then she investigated all the gardens in Pont-l'Évêque, and stopped the passers-by. "You don't ever happen to have seen my parrot, by any chance, do you?" And she gave a description of the parrot to those who did not know him. Suddenly, behind the mills at the foot of the hill she thought she could make out something green that fluttered. But on top of the hill there was nothing. A hawker assured her that he had come across the parrot just before, at Saint-Melaine, in Mère Simon's shop. She rushed there; they had no idea of what she meant. At last she came home exhausted, with her slippers in shreds and despair in her soul; and as she was sitting in the middle of the garden-seat at Madame's side, telling the whole story of her efforts, a light weight dropped on to her shoulder—it was Loulou! What on earth had he been doing? Taking a walk in the neighborhood, perhaps!

She had some trouble in recovering from this, or rather never did recover. As the result of a chill she had an attack of quinsy, and soon afterwards an earache. Three years later she was deaf; and she spoke very loud, even in church. Though Félicité's sins might have been published in every corner of the diocese without dishonor to her or scandal to anybody, his Reverence the priest thought it right now to hear her confession in the sacristy only.

Imaginary noises in the head completed her upset. Her mistress often said to hear, "Heavens! how stupid you are!" "Yes, Madame," she replied, and looked about for something.

Her little circle of ideas grew still narrower; the peal of church-bells and the lowing of cattle ceased to exist for her. All living beings moved as silently as ghosts. One sound only reached her ears now—the parrot's voice.

Loulou, as though to amuse her, reproduced the click-clack of the turn-spit, the shrill call of a man selling fish, and the noise of the saw in the joiner's house opposite; when the bell rang he imitated Mme. Aubain's "Félicité! the door! the door!"

They carried on conversations, he endlessly reciting the three phrases in his repertory, to which she replied with words that were just as disconnected but uttered what was in her heart. Loulou was almost a son and a lover to her in her isolated state. He climbed up her fingers, nibbled at her lips, and clung to her kerchief; and when she bent her forehead and shook her head gently to and fro, as nurses do, the great wings of her bonnet and the bird's wings quivered together.

When the clouds massed and the thunder rumbled Loulou broke into cries, perhaps remembering the downpours in his native forests. The streaming rain made him absolutely mad; he fluttered wildly about, dashed up to the ceiling, upset everything, and went out through the window to dabble in the garden; but he was back quickly to perch on one of the fire-dogs and hopped about to dry himself, exhibiting his tail and his beak in turn.

One morning in the terrible winter of 1837 she had put him in front of the fireplace because of the cold. She found him dead, in the middle of his cage: head downwards, with his claws in the wires. He had died from congestion, no doubt. But Félicité thought he had been poisoned with parsley, and though there was no proof of any kind her suspicions inclined to Fabu.

She wept so piteously that her mistress said to her, "Well, then, have him stuffed!"

She asked advice from the chemist, who had always been kind to the parrot. He wrote to Havre, and a person called Fellacher undertook the business. But as parcels sometimes got lost in the coach she decided to take the parrot as far as Honfleur herself.

Along the sides of the road were leafless apple-trees, one after the other. Ice covered the ditches. Dogs barked about the farms; and Félicité, with her hands under her cloak, her little black sabots and her basket, walked briskly in the middle of the road.

She crossed the forest, passed High Oak, and reached St. Gatien.

A cloud of dust rose behind her, and in it a mail-coach, carried away by the steep hill, rushed down at full gallop like a hurricane. Seeing this woman who would not get out of the way, the driver stood up in front and the postilion shouted too. He could not hold in his four horses, which increased their pace, and the two leaders were grazing her when he threw them to one side with a jerk of the reins. But he was wild with rage, and lifting his arm as he passed at full speed, gave her such a lash from waist to neck with his big whip that she fell on her back.

Her first act, when she recovered consciousness, was to open her basket. Loulou was happily none the worse. She felt a burn in her right cheek, and when she put her hands against it they were red; the blood was flowing.

She sat down on a heap of stones and bound up her face with her handkerchief. Then she ate a crust of bread which she had put in the basket as a precaution, and found a consolation for her wound in gazing at the bird.

When she reached the crest of Ecquemauville she saw the Honfleur lights sparkling in the night sky like a company of stars; beyond, the sea stretched dimly. Then a faintness overtook her and she stopped; her wretched childhood, the disillusion of her first love, her nephew's going away, and Virginie's death all came back to her at once like the waves of an oncoming tide, rose to her throat, and choked her.

Afterwards, at the boat, she make a point of speaking to the captain, begging him to take care of the parcel, though she did not tell him what was in it.

Fellacher kept the parrot a long time. He was always promising it for the following week. After six months he announced that a packing-case had started, and then nothing more was heard of it. It really seemed as though Loulou was never coming back. "Ah, they have stolen him!" she thought.

He arrived at last, and looked superb. There he was, erect upon a branch which screwed into a mahogany socket, with a foot in the air and his head on one side, biting a nut which the bird-stuffer—with a taste for impressiveness—had gilded.

Félicité shut him up in her room. It was a place to which few people were admitted, and held so many religious objects and miscellaneous things that it looked like a chapel and bazaar in one.

A big cupboard impeded you as you opened the door. Opposite the window commanding the garden a little round one looked into the court; there was a table by the folding-bed with a water-jug, two combs, and a cube of blue soap in a chipped plate. On the walls hung rosaries, medals, several benign Virgins, and a holy water vessel made out of cocoa-nut; on the chest of drawers, which was covered with a cloth like an altar, was the shell box that Victor had given her, and after that a watering-can, a toy-balloon, exercise-books, the illustrated geography, and a pair of young lady's boots; and, fastened by its ribbons to the nail of the looking-glass, hung the little plush hat! Félicité carried observances of this kind so far as to keep one of Monsieur's frock-coats. All the old rubbish which Mme. Aubain did not want any longer she laid hands on for her room. That was why there were artificial flowers along the edge of the chest of drawers and a portrait of the Comte d'Artois in the little window recess.

With the aid of a bracket Loulou was established over the chimney, which jutted into the room. Every morning when she woke up she saw him there in the dawning light, and recalled old days and the smallest details of insignificant acts in a deep quietness which knew no pain.

Holding, as she did, no communication with anyone, Félicité lived as insensibly as if she were walking in her sleep. The Corpus Christi processions roused her to life again. Then she went round begging mats and candlesticks from the neighbors to decorate the altar they put up in the street.

In church she was always gazing at the Holy Ghost in the window, and observed that there was something of the parrot in him. The likeness was still clearer, she thought, on a crude color-print representing the baptism of Our Lord. With his purple wings and emerald body he was the very image of Loulou.

She bought him, and hung him up instead of the Comte d'Artois, so that she could see them both together in one glance. They were linked in her thoughts; and the parrot was consecrated by his association with the Holy Ghost, which became more vivid to her eye and more intelligible. The Father could not have chosen to express Himself through a dove, for such creatures cannot speak; it must have been one of Loulou's ancestors, surely. And though Félicité looked at the picture while she said her prayers she swerved a little from time to time towards the parrot.

She wanted to join the Ladies of the Virgin, but Mme. Aubain dissuaded her.

And then a great event loomed up before them—Paul's marriage.

He had been a solicitor's clerk to begin with, and then tried business, the Customs, the Inland Revenue, and made efforts, even, to get into the Rivers and Forests. By an inspiration from heaven he had suddenly, at thirty-six, discovered his real line—the Registrar's Office. And there he showed such marked capacity that an inspector had offered him his daughter's hand and promised him his influence.

So Paul, grown serious, brought the lady to see his mother.

She sniffed at the ways of Pont-l'Évêque, gave herself great airs, and wounded Félicité's feelings. Mme. Aubain was relieved at her departure.

The week after came news of M. Bourais' death in an inn in Lower Brittany. The rumor of suicide was confirmed, and doubts arose as to his honesty. Mme. Aubain studied his accounts, and soon found out the whole tale of his misdoings—embezzled arrears, secret sales of wood, forged receipts, etc. Besides that he had an illegitimate child, and "relations with a person at Dozulé."

These shameful facts distressed her greatly. In March 1853 she was seized with a pain in the chest; her tongue seemed to be covered with film, and leeches did not ease the difficult breathing. On the ninth evening of her illness she died, just at seventy-two.

She passed as being younger, owing to the bands of brown hair which framed her pale, pock-marked face. There were few friends to regret her, for she had a stiffness of manner which kept people at a distance.

But Félicité mourned for her as one seldom mourns for a master. It upset her ideas and seemed contrary to the order of things, impossible and monstrous, that Madame should die before her.

Ten days afterwards, which was the time it took to hurry there from Besançon, the heirs arrived. The daughter-in-law ransacked the drawers, chose some furniture, and sold the rest; and then they went back to their registering.

Madame's armchair, her small round table, her foot-warmer, and the eight chairs were gone! Yellow patches in the middle of the panels showed where the engravings had hung. They had carried off the two little beds and the mattresses, and all Virginie's belongings had disappeared from the cupboard. Félicité went from floor to floor dazed with sorrow.

The next day there was a notice on the door, and the apothecary shouted in her ear that the house was for sale.

She tottered, and was obliged to sit down. What distressed her most of all was to give up her room, so suitable as it was for poor Loulou. She enveloped him with a look of anguish when she was imploring the Holy Ghost, and formed the idolatrous habit of kneeling in front of the parrot to say her prayers. Sometimes the sun shone in at the attic window and caught his glass eye, and a great luminous ray shot out of it and put her in an ecstasy.

She had a pension of fifteen pounds a year which her mistress had left her. The garden gave her a supply of vegetables. As for clothes, she had enough to last her to the end of her days, and she economized in candles by going to bed at dusk.

She hardly ever went out, as she did not like passing the dealer's shop, where some of the old furniture was exposed for sale. Since her fit of giddiness she dragged one leg; and as her strength was failing Mère Simon, whose grocery business had collapsed, came every morning to split the wood and pump water for her.

Her eyes grew feeble. The shutters ceased to be thrown open. Years and years passed, and the house was neither let nor sold.

Félcité never asked for repairs because she was afraid of being sent away. The boards on the roof rotted; her bolster was wet for a whole winter. After Easter she spat blood.

Then Mère Simon called in a doctor. Félicité wanted to know what was the matter with her. But she was too deaf to hear, and the only word which reached her was "pneumo-nia." It was a word she knew, and she answered softly "Ah! like Madame," thinking it natural that she should follow her mistress.

The time for the festal shrines was coming near. The first one was always at the bottom of the hill, the second in front of the post-office, and the third towards the middle of the street. There was some rivalry in the matter of this one, and the women of the parish ended by choosing Mme. Aubain's courtyard.

The hard breathing and fever increased. Félicité was vexed at doing nothing for the altar. If only she could at least have put something there! Then she thought of the parrot.

The neighbors objected that it would not be decent. But the priest gave her permission, which so intensely delighted her that she begged him to accept Loulou, her sole possession, when she died.

From Tuesday to Saturday, the eve of the festival, she coughed more often. By the evening her face had shriveled, her lips stuck to her gums, and she had vomitings; and at twilight next morning, feeling herself very low, she sent for a priest.

Three kindly women were round her during the extreme unction. Then she announced that she must speak to Fabu. He arrived in his Sunday clothes, by no means at his ease in the funereal atmosphere.

"Forgive me," she said, with an effort to stretch out her arm; "I thought it was you who had killed him."

What did she mean by such stories? She suspected him of murder—a man like him! He waxed indignant, and was on the point of making a row.

"There," said the women, "she is no longer in her senses, you can see it well enough!"

Félicité spoke to shadows of her own from time to time. The women went away, and Mère Simon had breakfast. A little later she took Loulou and brought him close to Félicité with the words:

"Come, now, say good-bye to him!"

Loulou was not a corpse, but the worms devoured him; one of his wings was broken, and the tow was coming out of his stomach. But she was blind now; she kissed him on the forehead and kept him close against her cheek. Mère Simon took him back from her to put him on the altar.

V

Summer scents came up from the meadows; flies buzzed; the sun made the river glitter and heated the slates. Mère Simon came back into the room and fell softly asleep.

She woke at the noise of bells; the people were coming out from vespers. Félicité's delirium subsided. She thought of the procession and saw it as if she had been there.

All the school children, the church-singers, and the firemen walked on the pavement, while in the middle of the road the verger armed with his hallebard and the beadle with a large cross advanced in front. Then came the schoolmaster, with an eye on the boys, and the sister, anxious about her little girls; three of the daintiest, with angelic curls, scattered rosepetals in the air; the deacon controlled the band with outstretched arms; and two censer-bearers turned back at every step towards the Holy Sacrament, which was borne by Monsieur the curé, wearing his beautiful chasuble, under a canopy of dark-red velvet held up by four churchwardens. A crowd of people pressed behind, between the white cloths covering the house walls, and they reached the bottom of the hill.

A cold sweat moistened Félicité's temples. Mère Simon sponged her with a piece of linen, saying to herself that one day she would have to go that way.

The hum of the crowd increased, was very loud for an instant, and then went further away.

A fusillade shook the window-panes. It was the postilions saluting the monstrance. Félicité rolled her eyes and said as audibly as she could: "Does he look well?" The parrot was weighing on her mind.

Her agony began. A death-rattle that grew more and more convulsed made her sides heave. Bubbles of froth came at the corners of her mouth and her whole body trembled.

Soon the booming of the ophicleides, the high voices of the children, and the deep voices of the men were distinguishable. At intervals all was silent, and the tread of feet, deadened by the flowers they walked on, sounded like a flock pattering on grass.

The clergy appeared in the courtyard. Mère Simon clambered on to a chair to reach the attic window, and so looked down straight upon the shrine. Green garlands hung over the altar, which was decked with a flounce of English lace. In the middle was a small frame with relics in it; there were two orange-trees at the corners, and all along stood silver candlesticks and china vases, with sunflowers, lilies, peonies, foxgloves, and tufts of hortensia. This heap of blazing color slanted from the level of the altar to the carpet which went on over the pavement; and some rare objects caught the eye. There was a silvergilt sugar-basin with a crown of violets; pendants of Alençon stone glittered on the moss, and two Chinese screens displayed their landscapes. Loulou was hidden under roses, and showed nothing but his blue forehead, like a plaque of lapis lazuli.

The churchwardens, singers, and children took their

places round the three sides of the court. The priest went slowly up the steps, and placed his great, radiant golden sun upon the lace. Everyone knelt down. There was a deep silence; and the censers glided to and fro on the full swing of their chains.

An azure vapor rose up into Félicité's room. Her nostrils met it; she inhaled it sensuously, mystically; and then closed her eyes. Her lips smiled. The beats of her heart lessened one by one, vaguer each time and softer, as a fountain sinks, an echo disappears; and when she sighed her last breath she thought she saw an opening in the heavens, and a gigantic parrot hovering above her head.